I0589179

PRAISE FOR ENTROMANCY: BOOK ONE OF THE NIGHTPATH TRILOGY

"Entromancy is that rare gem you find among the all-too-common dross of self-published novels. Author M. S. Farzan takes a premise that is truly unique and imaginative . . . throws in a diverse cast of characters, all to deliver an urban fantasy thrill ride."

--San Francisco Book Review

"In this rousing...science fiction novel, it's a futuristic San Francisco and the element [c]eridium has emerged as a renewed source of mythical power and otherworldly strength. Ceridium's side-effects, however, unlock mutative genes in the population resulting in a secondary race called [a]urics who become threatening to the human population. Thankfully, vigilant cops like Eskander Aradowsi are defending the races and reinforcing the safety of each. The narrative is fast-paced...this is a promising...launching point for the planned series."

--The BookLife Prize in Fiction

"Entromancy has been an amazing journey...which I think I would like to take again

in the next book of the Nightpath Trilogy. The world building is out of this world no pun intended. If you like a lot of action, fighting and guns a blazing then you are going to fall in love with this series."

--The Avid Reader

"ENTROMANCY has one of the coolest speculative fiction worlds I've encountered in a while. The mix of magic and technology is an amazing blend that results in all kind of badassery from the characters. Backdropped against a sort of dystopian/Philip Marlow-ian cityscape, it felt like an epic D&D slipstream universe...I recommend this book for anyone who wants to get lost in an awesome world and/or anyone who grew up on table-top role-playing games."

--Kit 'N Kabookle

"I love all the characters in the book...I love the little hint of romance that floats in the plot while everyone get shot at. I really couldn't put this book down once it got started."

--Emily Carrington

"This book was a fun to read story that centered on several important issues concerning diversity, differences, and deeply-held fears. I read mostly to be entertained, but I couldn't help but think about some of problems in terms of today's

political climate. An attention-grabbing tale of conspiracy, hatred, and misconceptions that was easy to read, fresh, and frightening, my reading time was well-spent with this book."

--Laurie's Paranormal Thoughts and Reviews

"I am in love with the worldbuilding on this one. Seriously, it's amazing. It's hard to write science fiction with fantasy races and have it make sense, but by jove, I have now seen it done...I'd recommend picking this up if you like a good mix of science fiction and fantasy."

--Where Landsquid Fear to Tread

"I enjoyed the story a great deal...The plot was tense and also topical, which was a great boon to the book. I liked the way that current events were used to see a new race and a new world order."

--Judge, 25th Annual Writer's Digest Self-Published Book Awards

"Very vivid...Very compelling...Very fresh and punchy"

--Judge, 5th Annual Writer's Digest Self-Published eBook Awards

PRAISE FOR ENTROMANCY: A CYBERPUNK FANTASY RPG

"An agile little assassin...Entromancy is a gem waiting to be found."

--Geek Native

"I am seriously impressed with this book. My favorite part is the near-total absence of scaling, and the menu-option approach to gaining new features from your class and destiny. It works well here for the same reason it works well in Powered by the Apocalypse playbooks and 13th Age."

--Tribality

"Nightpath [Publishing] has established a setting with teeth that can grab the imagination of player and game master."

--EN World

"A...cyberpunk/fantasy take on the 5E rules that might be one of the fastest pick-up-and-play games out there."

--Drop Lowest

BOOKS BY M. S. FARZAN

Entromancy: Book One of the Nightpath Trilogy
Technomancy: Book Two of the Nightpath Trilogy
Shadowmancy: Book Three of the Nightpath Trilogy
Jinnspeak

GAMES BY M. S. FARZAN

Entromancy: A Cyberpunk Fantasy RPG
Entromancy: Hacker Battles
Not-So-Super Villains

ENTROMANCY

BOOK ONE OF THE NIGHTPATH TRILOGY

M. S. Farzan

For Mom, Dad, and Annie
My world, which inspires me to write about
others

ACKNOWLEDGEMENTS

The act of writing may by nature be a solitary endeavor, but it is rarely done in a vacuum. I am deeply indebted to my parents, to Andrea, and to Brian, for their infinite patience in editing, critiquing, suggesting, supporting, listening, reviewing, and unfailingly, reading. I am also appreciative of Meredith's incredible eye for design and generosity with innumerable proofs, and thankful for the work of Elena, Kat, and Owen in creating the art for new covers. Additionally, I am grateful for my monthly gaming group and best friends besides, who provide for some of the most ridiculous scenarios, which in turn spur the imagination to consider the most epic of stories.

In addition to the above dedication, this book is for anyone who has ever felt marginalized, isolated, or alienated for being different.

PROLOGUE

Tribe hummed to himself cheerily as he worked the clothes hanger through the tiny crack. Slender olive fingers probed expertly at the window base, dexterously seeking the catch that would spring the sedan's passenger door.

"Any day now," he complained, feeling the metal slip along the inside of the door. Slowly, he slid the hanger from one side of the window to the other, nudging the antiquated locking mechanism within.

After what seemed like an eternity, the hanger caught on a thick piece of metal, and Tribe shifted his grip, carefully pulling on the catch without unraveling the hanger's hook.

"Easy," he cautioned himself.

Confident with the hanger's position, the auric gave it a quick tug. The catch sprung abruptly, giving way under the sudden pressure, and unlocked the door with a faint click.

"Ace," he breathed triumphantly, withdrawing the hanger silently and stowing it within a ratty knapsack. Taking a cursory look around him, he opened the car door and slid inside, shifting uncomfortably over the ancient gearshift and into the driver's seat. As he suspected, the prehistoric machine had the most rudimentary of controls, without boosters or touch recognition. Apart from what appeared to be a more modern stereo system, the car's interior looked like something found in a VR museum tour, although it was in much worse shape. The antique still ran on electricity.

Tribe pulled a digitab from his jacket and held it up to the ignition button, syncing the device with the car's primitive computer. He tapped a few buttons and the sedan purred to life, humming softly as its console lit up with LEDs. Swiping through a few screens, he found the machine's stereo system, and synced it with the device's prized music supply. A turn-of-the-century hip hop track buzzed through the antiquated speakers, gently vibrating the car frame.

"Not bad," the thief nodded to himself. Checking his side mirror, he put the sedan in gear while waiting for an opening in the nighttime traffic. Neon lights assailed his sensitive eyes as cars zipped past and above him, and he had to squint just to see the street behind him. After a brief wait, there was a short lull in the lower traffic, and he pulled the small vehicle into the roadway, immediately slamming his foot down on the acceleration pedal to blend into the flow of cars.

Speeding as quickly as the old sedan would let him, he made his way through SOMA and into downtown, ignoring the periodic flicker of blue lights overhead as the boostered vehicles passed above him. He slowed as he reached a traffic light, drawing an Oxidium packet from a pocket and slipping one of the small pellets into his mouth. The drug immediately took effect, clearing his vision and seeming to slow down everything around him. He tapped impatiently on the steering wheel in time with the music as the light ahead took agonizingly slow to turn.

As if in slow motion, the red light turned green, but Tribe's heightened senses led him to notice a bit of motion out of the corner of his eye. Four NIGHT cruisers sped through the intersection's bottom and upper levels, siren lights flashing silently and blue light spilling from their ceridium engine vents. Cars around and above him pulled up nervously to avoid hitting them and each other.

"Someone's in a hurry," Tribe said to no one in particular as he watched the agents speed away.

*****

Karthax stood on the balcony, holding the digitab out in front of him. A sandy beach stretched out below, the Atlantic a sparkling blanket of jewels beyond. A balmy breeze caressed his dry skin, lightly ruffling his military fatigues.

"The wheels are set," he spoke into the device. "Expect my call within the week."

The figure on the digitab display grunted in agreement. "And if it fails?"

"That will not happen," Karthax reassured him. The Inquisitor General paced along the balcony rail, the sun casting his craggy face in radiance.

"I require more than your personal guarantees," the figure replied.

Expecting the skepticism, Karthax had his answer prepared. "The Destroyer will work for us on this."

"The Betrayer does not work for anyone but himself," the figure corrected him.

The Inquisitor General swatted at a fly buzzing near his face. "Nonetheless, he has agreed to perform any necessary cleanup."

The figure considered Karthax's words for a moment, long enough to make the human wonder if his display had frozen. Then it grunted again in agreement.

"I will await your call."

The digitab clicked, and the display went black. Karthax pocketed the device, putting his burly forearms on the balcony railing and gazing out at the horizon. Below, the ocean lapped lazily at the quiet beach, tracing sparkling foam patterns in the sand.

*****

Thog'run II handed the digitab to an advisor, settling back into his throne. The king put his hand on the large battleaxe resting against his leg, rocking it absently against the stone floor.

"Sire, if I may," the advisor said politely, "it feels as though we have made a deal with the devil."

Thog'run stared ahead, his calculating eyes piercing the dim light of the underground audience chamber. A guard shifted nervously nearby, uncomfortable with being privy to the conversation.

"It does feel that way, doesn't it," the auric king said.

ONE

The NIGHTs are excellent strategists, combatants, and mancers, but they have a singular vision of the world and its inhabitants. Would that they would see less black and white and more grey.

-The Sigil of Sparks

"How many out there?" a voice buzzed through my earpiece.

I watched the city below carefully, standing stock still as the evening breeze whipped my coat behind me. The bright neon lights formed an iridescent halo through the layer of fog that had begun to coalesce, but I could still pinpoint a handful of signal markers within the haze. The ancient radio tower loomed behind me forlornly like a ruddy tuning fork sticking out of a concrete mound.

I tapped a button on my digitab, magnifying a selected portion of the cityscape through my lenses. "Three," I replied. "Two on Columbus-Farrow and one downtown."

"Pissing underrats."

I grimaced at the racism, but said nothing. Marking the three waypoints on my digitab's city map, I hurried back to the cruiser bike.

"HQ wants you to prioritize the downtown storefront," the voice continued. "Intel says that it's set to go nova first, and there's no telling what these gutter trash will do when we expose them."

I nodded to myself as I mounted the cruiser, passing a gloved hand over the vehicle's blinking security console. Its engine instantly came to life, cold blue light spilling out of the bike's casing.

"Oh and, Nightpath," my earpiece buzzed. "Bring me a couple of knife-ears as souvenirs, will you?"

I tensed on the bike, disgusted by the snickering I could hear in the background.

"That's enough, Striker," I said curtly.

The laughter stopped abruptly. "Just get it done," the voice said, and the earpiece clicked.

"Jackass," I spat, irritably flicking a dial on the bike's handlebar. The cruiser jolted forward under my touch like an angry dog against a leash, the ceridium engine growling mutedly beneath me. I spun the bike in a quick u-turn and began making my way down the barren hill back to Old Market and the downtown signal marker.

The city was unseasonably warm, a sinking,

dry heat that was only just being chased away by the fog. It had been a hot week, the one handful of days out of the year that the temperature came anywhere close to triple digits. I was sweating under my standard issue uniform and long coat, my hands damp against the cruiser's metal grips. The neighborhood around me, no more than abandoned houses and empty lots this far up Twin Peaks, smelled of dirt and old pavement.

I checked the time in the corner of my lens display, which read 20:31:59. I had over an hour to get to the downtown location, more than enough time to neutralize the situation and make my way to North Beach. The storefronts, which represented over two months of undercover stakeouts, bribes, and interrogation by questionable means - what the NIGHT leadership liked to call "careful research" - represented the tip of an iceberg. A couple of tiny first-floor shops rigged to blow were nothing compared to the extensive terrorist network that was teeming beneath the city, and defusing them was no more than a lame PR move to demonstrate that the government's pet protection agency still had jurisdiction at the civic level. As much as I hated to admit it, Striker was right about one thing: no one quite knew what the revs would do when they were exposed.

Tall, dimly lit apartment buildings began to

dot the sides of the road as I made my way out of Twin Peaks and down Old Market. The project housing, which had been hastily built after the establishment of Aurichome to support the massive influx of human refugees, was an eyesore on what was otherwise a potentially picturesque landscape. Here and there, between the increasingly numerous buildings, I caught glimpses of the luminous city below, bustling with nighttime activity. I swerved between the few cars that were on the road this far away from the city center, accelerating as I neared the first row of neon-encrusted structures.

The change in architecture as I reached New Castro was as abrupt as it was symbolic, signifying a shift in population as well as resources. Old money had met new money on the outskirts of the city center and they both liked their nice things. Rows of erstwhile apartment buildings had been reclaimed and repurposed as nightclubs, VR emporiums, and vacation houses for the handful of moguls who had made a killing on the augmented reality media boom. Dozens of digads assaulted my senses as I sped through the vibrant neighborhood, pulsing asynchronously from AR-enabled monitors in front of each storefront.

The lower nighttime traffic increased considerably as I cruised through the busy district, slowing to a crawl as I reached the New

Castro-downtown border. Tapping a few buttons on the cruiser's console, I engaged the vehicle's boosters, gently revving the ceridium engine and easing into the less congested upper tier.

From my new vantage point, I could easily see through the fog of AR animations and into downtown, and began to review the mission briefing from memory. The NIGHT intel had identified three underrace-owned storefronts that were emptied out and rigged to blow within fifteen minutes of each other. They were thought to be distractions from whatever scheme the revolutionaries had planned this time, which was undoubtedly above my pay grade.

I made a face, disgusted with how the NIGHT leadership and the government at large had let it get to this point. Locking people up, taking away their basic rights, and treating them as second-class citizens had always proven to be a surefire way to foment revolt. Remove everything they have to believe in, and they'll make every effort to return the favor.

The worst part was the lack of any kind of accountability on the NIGHT leadership and politicians behind the current state of affairs. Any questions about the maltreatment of auric prisoners or rights talk in general would be unfailingly met with vague statements about internal defense, or even worse, feigned ignorance about the root cause of revolutionary violence, with some sideways remark about the rage plague and the need for greater Oxidium control.

I shook my head and refocused on the task at hand. By all accounts, it would be a standard breaking and entering job with minimal force; defuse the bomb and neutralize any hostiles. The NIGHT headquarters would dispatch heavier forces to the other two storefronts, which would undoubtedly see more resistance when the first place didn't blow as planned. I'd be in and out in under ten minutes, tops.

I slowed slightly as I made my way deeper into the downtown district, which was no less colorful than New Castro with its towering, digad-pocked buildings that crowded together as if huddling against the fog encroaching from the Bay. Turning onto a small side street, I disengaged the cruiser's boosters and coasted to the bottom level. The shift was almost deafening in its marked decrease in traffic noise and digads, with only a few trucks loading and unloading at service entrances and a few street people making their way through the night.

I checked my location against the signal marker that I had observed from the old radio tower, nodding to myself. If the NIGHTs' informants were being paid the right amount, the signal marker they had set up would correctly lead me to a storefront two blocks away, without any paper or digital trail to identify them to the revs' leadership. The auric king's people didn't take kindly to snitches.

I turned into a tiny cul-de-sac, passing a hand over the cruiser's console to turn off the engine. I stepped off of the vehicle and unraveled my long coat, adjusting my lenses to see better in the dim light away from the main thoroughfare. Moving casually but silently, I walked to the mouth of the alley and peered down the side street towards the storefront, a large corner location masquerading as a legalized Oxidium dispensary. Unlike the larger buildings surrounding it, the shop was comprised of only two stories, with dark, nondescript windows facing out towards the intersection.

Reaching into a pocket, I opened a small packet and slipped a ceridium capsule into my hand. I held it out in front of me and made several deft, practiced gestures, scanning the street around me to ensure that I wasn't drawing any undue attention. With a final pass of my hand, I crushed the capsule and tossed the contents over my head in a brief flash of blue. I could feel my skin tingling slightly as the spell took effect, shrouding me in a gentle mist that would hide me from all but direct eye contact.

I quietly padded down the street towards the

location's opposing corner, filtering the different readings coming through my lenses and being recorded onto my digitab. A handful of night porters were working a block away, loading furniture into a large truck. Two street people slept under the cover of an awning, bundled even during the unusual heat. Several parked cars lined the roadway, all but one appearing cold in the IR scan. From my vantage, the storefront looked quiet and empty, as expected.

The timer on the upper corner of my lens display read 21:04:05, forty-one minutes before the place was set to blow. Plenty of time.

Giving the adjacent buildings a quick scan, I briskly walked across the street towards the back entrance of the dispensary, around the corner from the storefront. I sized up the wall in front of me, delicately placing a foot upon a jutting piece of stucco and using it to spring up towards a second-story window sill. I grabbed the sill with one hand and used my feet against the wall for balance, confident that if anyone happened to look my way from an appreciable distance, they'd see no more than a nondescript smudge on the wall.

Using my free hand, I pried at the window, feeling it give way easily under my touch. I opened it silently, gliding through the opening and into a long, unlit hallway that smelled heavily of damp wood and unwashed bodies. Several doorways opened into the corridor, with a stairwell at the far end that presumably led down into the Oxidium dispensary.

It took me all of two seconds to notice that something was wrong. I could hear soft sounds coming from the rooms opening off the hall, and a faint light flickered from the chamber closest to the stairs. I moved down the corridor and sidled up against the first doorway, trusting in my shadow shroud to keep me hidden from all but the most observant of spectators. I ducked my head in and out of the room, allowing my lenses to record its contents.

I felt my breath catch in my throat, and a terrible premonition began to snake its way through my subconscious. Hurrying to the next doorway, I quickly peered inside and felt my stomach tighten in response, either from the overpowering smell, anxiety, or both.

I crept back towards the open window, scrolling through my digitab to find the right contact and tapping a button.

"The hell you want, Nightpath?" Striker's voice greeted me after a few beeps. "Don't you have a job to do?"

"Piss off, Striker," I retorted through clenched teeth. "Downtown doesn't match briefing intel. There are people here, a lot of them, all ragers."

"The hell does that matter? Do the job, man."

"Damn it, Striker!" I clipped, looking around me to make sure I still hadn't been noticed.

"I'm saying it doesn't make sense. Why would the revs blow up their own?"

"You get paid to ask questions, or you get paid to shoot people?" Striker's voice buzzed. "Do the job."

"Not innocents, prick!" I could feel my patience dissipating into anger. "Listen to me, Striker. There are *kids* in here. Something's not right."

"Do the job, Nightpath," Striker repeated, and the digitab clicked.

I growled incoherently at the closed line, taking another cursory look around me and noting the time. 21:12:04.

"Piss."

Two rooms were filled to the brim with people in various states of consciousness, vibrant in my lenses' IR spectrum with the telltale fever of the rage plague. Aurics mostly, with a few humans here and there tending to them or keeping them company. Adults, children, elderly, young. By the size and number of rooms, I'd estimate over fifty people sedated and being held on the brink of lunacy.

"Piss," I said again. The revolutionaries were known for their guerilla tactics and tenacity, not for their brutality. If the building was set to explode, the auric king would have blood of his own kind on his hands, which signified a new depth to his desire to control the city. It was a big play, but it didn't change my objective.

I pocketed my digitab and crept down the corridor, back towards the stairwell. The building was stifling, hotter than the outside world with no hint of a breeze. I could feel a nervous sweat dampen my clothes under my arms and at the small of my back. I sidled past several other rooms and approached the lighted room next to the stairs. A faint murmuring drifted out from it and into the corridor.

Just as I reached the room's open doorway, a tall auric dressed in street clothes and dangling with piercings walked out of the room, head down as he counted a wad of crumpled paper money. "Later," he called over his shoulder as he turned the corner and trotted down the stairwell, oblivious to my presence.

I waited several beats until I heard a door close downstairs. Peering around the corner and into the room, I could clearly make out several figures in the dim light, my brown eyes picking up on tusks and horns while my lenses picked up the rest. Five aurics, all conscious, with no signs of the rage plague. Two human-sized pairs sitting at as many tables, with one gigantic troll of an auric propped up against a corner wall, all absorbed in their digitabs, which provided the room's only meager illumination. Their superior vision wouldn't need any more than that.

I pressed my back against the wall, mentally preparing myself for what was next. I didn't have time for a protracted battle, and the stakes had just become infinitely higher with the presence of innocent people. Shaking my coat sleeve to drop a long dart from my forearm holster into my left palm, I drew my ceridium-powered stunner into my right. Finesse would have to take precedence over firepower, or I'd have a building full of ragers on me in no time.

I took a short breath and looked at my time display. 21:16:34.

I turned the corner and unleashed chaos into the room.

Spinning through the doorway, I allowed my shadow shroud to curl and coalesce around me, throwing the dart across my body towards the troll, who was just looking up from his digitab. The hulk caught the projectile in the side of his neck, slumping instantaneously from the tranquilizer. Simultaneously, I emptied the stunner's two rounds at the aurics directly to my left. One of them raised an arm reflexively and caught the electrified bolt in a brawny forearm, jittering and falling to the wood floor with a muted thump. The other, a bit more unlucky, took the round in the face and fell backwards, hitting his head on the side of a chair.

The other two responded immediately, reaching for cobalt-glowing handguns within their heavy jackets. I holstered the stunner and darted towards them, jumping and twisting while grabbing another ceridium capsule from my billowing coat. I caught the closest one squarely in the jaw with a thrust from my boot, landing just as the other stood up from her chair and leveled her gun at my twirling form. I came out of my spin and grabbed the auric's wrist, twisting the weapon expertly from her hand and locking her arm against my body. As she opened her mouth to shout, I spoke a word of power and crushed the capsule in my hand, tossing the blue dust into her face and rendering her instantly unconscious.

I let the auric's body slip heavily back into the chair, and glanced at the time. 21:17:02. Twenty-eight minutes.

"What are you trying to play, man?" a voice reverberated from the hallway. "We said five hundred, not..."

The voice trailed off as I turned around back towards the door. The pierced auric had returned, standing in the doorway with his eyes wide open and his mouth frozen in mid-sentence. It must have been an impressive scene, with me standing like a cloak of death amid the carnage. The man on the floor spasmed awkwardly, latent electricity charging through his body.

"The hell?" the auric said, bewildered.

I moved, and he saw me. My lenses magnified his dilated pupils, and registered his slightly elevated pulse and shallow breaths.

The Oxidium would have enhanced his already superior vision, and improved his reflexes to a near super-human level.

I took a step towards him, which spurred him out of his daze, and he dashed out of the doorway towards the stairwell. I raced after him, vaulting towards the door and grabbing the frame to swing around the corner. The stairs switched back upon themselves, and the auric's heightened speed had already taken him to the little landing in between the two floors. I jumped lightly upon the railing that bisected the stairwell, and used my momentum to carry me over the switchback.

I landed upon the auric's back like a cloud of smoke, snaking my arms around his neck and under his armpit like a vise. He lost his footing under the added weight and we tumbled down the remaining stairs, crashing through a light wooden door and knocking into a small stack of empty cardboard boxes. I rolled with the impact and held onto his neck and arm, clenching like a python as he tried to wriggle away from me. The spikes on his leather jacket poked through my coat and tore at my arms, but I ignored the pain and locked a foot around the crook of his knee to try to arch my back for more leverage.

The auric threw his head backwards, catching me cleanly in the temple. My grip loosened on him as stars exploded in my head, and I could feel him scrambling amidst the boxes as he tried to escape. I reached out a hand reflexively and caught at his leg, managing to grab a handful of his trousers. I pulled and twisted, knocking him off balance and back to the floor.

Instinctively, I rolled out of the way, and was rewarded by catching his hi-top sneaker on my shoulder instead of my face. I swatted at it with one hand and used the other to push myself into a crouch, shaking my vision clear and willing myself to stay conscious. I sensed him getting to his feet and saw a flash in my peripheral vision. I ducked underneath his kick and sprung up from the floor, driving the crown of my head into his chin. His teeth came together with an audible crack, and he fell to the floor like a bag of groceries.

"Jesus!" he exclaimed meekly, clutching at his jaw. "You broke my tongue!"

I ignored him, shaking my head again and surveying the chamber. It was a little storage area that opened up into the storefront proper, which was essentially one large room with a long bar that ran from one end to the other. A couple of digital registers sat on the otherwise unremarkable counter, and small cabinets marked with augmented reality-enabled writing lined the adjacent wall. A soft light penetrated through the room's windows from the street.

My head swam a little, and I looked at the time, dropping the shadow shroud. 21:21:52.

"Come on," I said to the auric, who was still writhing on the ground. I grabbed a handful of hair and dragged him into the empty room, irritated by the interruption to my mission and wary of any further complications. The auric's piercings jangled, his jacket spikes scratching at the wood floor.

Even without the lenses' readout, it would have been easy to spot the bomb if one knew what they were looking for. I noticed it immediately, nestled in between two chairs that were bolted into the wall on the far side of the room, out of sight from anyone who might happen to have access to the dispensary after hours. I strode around the bar towards it, pulling the auric behind me.

"The hell, man! I didn't do anything!" he said, struggling weakly against me. "Let me go!"

I squatted in between the chairs and put my knee on the auric's throat to keep him from squirming. He seemed to accept his situation and slumped in defeat. I pulled my digitab out of my coat and set it against the bomb, tapping a few buttons to sync with the device. It was a tiny thing, the size of a roach or VPen chip, but placed expertly at the base of a load-bearing wall. When it blew, it would take the entire building with it.

The digitab finished syncing, displaying information about the bomb's specifications and a defuse protocol. It was Canadian made, and a newer model at that - no more than a year old. The ticker on it read six minutes and forty-two seconds, a full thirteen minutes before it was supposed to go off.

I felt a bead of sweat trickle down my forehead, the dark room closing in oppressively around me. My temple throbbed, and I could feel the adrenaline of combat slipping away from my body, leaving a hollow feeling of uncertainty in the pit of my stomach. I licked my lips nervously and clicked on the defuse protocol, which opened up a code prompt. I quickly entered the combination provided to me during the mission briefing, which would stop the countdown and disable the bomb.

The digitab buzzed angrily, indicating that the combination I had entered was either incorrect or had been changed. The ticker burped, knocking a minute off the timer and now reading four minutes and twenty-two seconds.

I fought to stay calm. I could hear my pulse pounding in my ears, matching the drumming in my temple, and I kept forgetting to breathe. I hedged, knowing that I could leave, taking the auric with me for questioning, but I wouldn't have time to evacuate the people upstairs. I wasn't familiar with being unsure of my next course of action, and I didn't care for the feeling.

I had neither the time to give the defuse protocol another try nor the skillset to hack into the device and do it the hard way. I synced the timer with my digitab and saw the countdown appear in my lenses. Pocketing the digitab, I released my knee from the auric's throat and grabbed him by the collar.

"What's the code?" I snarled at him.

"What?" he said thickly. I could see the blood staining his white teeth.

"Don't play stupid with me," I said, shaking him. "What's the code?"

"The hell, man? What code?"

I could see that he had no idea what I was talking about. I glanced back at the bomb and up at the time display. 21:27:24, three minutes and thirty-six seconds.

The auric craned his neck to follow my gaze, then looked at me. I could see understanding register in his eyes.

"We're dead?" he queried.

I nodded absently, reaching for another ceridium capsule. Prying off a glove with my teeth, I reached out towards the device.

The auric's hand shot up and grabbed weakly at my wrist. "You're going to kill us, man!" he protested.

"Probably!" I looked back towards a side entrance next to the counter. "Can you open that?"

He hesitated, then nodded slightly.

"Do it," I said. He got up slowly and trotted over to the door.

I returned my attention to the bomb, and delicately pried at it with my fingers. It was stuck firmly to the wall with some kind of adhesive, but I picked at it with a fingernail gently, making sure not to damage the device itself.

"The *hell*, man," I heard the auric behind me. "You made me lose my keys!"

"Be creative!" I yelled back, and could hear movement upstairs. Our little row must have woken up some of the ragers. I didn't have time to savor the irony of my attempt to save the lives of a group of people who would be happy to tear me apart at the slightest provocation.

I continued picking at the device, absently wiping my forehead with my free hand. It came away bloody. I ignored the pain in my temple and gave the bomb another flick, and it fell into my palm with a little resistance.

I hastily moved my other hand around the device in a circular motion, chanting softly under my breath and crushing the ceridium capsule. A shadowy thread, almost invisible in the darkness, emanated from my fingers, building upon itself and wrapping around the bomb like a ball of black yarn. I closed my fist over it and ran back towards the counter.

The time in my lens display read 21:30:28. Thirty-two seconds.

Muttering to himself, the auric was working at the door's physical locking mechanism with a pair of picks, having already disabled the digital keycode. I shouldered him out of the way and drew my ceridium pistol, stepping back and firing a round into the deadbolt. It blew a baseball-sized hole through the door with a loud *whoosh* and the lock went with it, leaving a smoking blue ring behind.

I ripped open the door and tossed the shadow-encrusted bomb into the street, aiming for a car across the asphalt. I barely had enough time to see it crash through the sedan's window, providing the neighborhood with the most meager of protection along with the shadow shield. I slammed the door against the frame, turning towards the auric and pushing him underneath the counter, shielding him with my body.

21:31:00.

The world exploded.

A light brighter than the sun flashed outside of the dispensary, illuminating the room with a painful flash. A dragon's roar filled my ears as the building shook, glass and bits of wood and plaster raining down painfully on my coat as the windows and parts of the walls blew. The ground rocked violently, threatening to tumble the entire dispensary down upon us. I could hear the auric yelling in fear below me.

Then, as soon as they had begun, the light and noise vanished. My ears rung in the silence, and I could taste blood in my mouth, having bitten my lip during the explosion. I held my position for several heartbeats, feeling the dust continue to rain down on me and waiting for the building to collapse.

Nothing happened. The whole neighborhood seemed to have fallen silent, as if waiting for someone to make the next move. Even the ragers upstairs seemed to have been temporarily mollified.

I dared to look up from my crouch, shaking woodchips and glass from my hair. The dispensary looked like it had been hit by a mortar, but it was still standing. The side door had been torn completely off of its hinges, and the glass double doors at the front of the building had shattered along with the windows. The wall closest to the side door had gaping holes where it had taken the brunt of the blast, but it held. I tried not to think of what the outside neighborhood looked like.

A million different scenarios came to my mind, hazy explanations for how a relatively easy job could have gone south so quickly. I pushed them out of my head, grateful for the moment just to be alive. I slumped against the counter, putting a hand to my temple and letting a long breath out through my nose. The auric crept up next to me, tentatively peering over the bar at the carnage.

"Jesus," he said.

TWO

The city is home to all of us, and we are entrusted with its protection. Nothing will sway us from that course.
  -William D. Karthax, NIGHT Inquisitor General

After a couple of seconds making sure I was still alive, I dusted the pieces of building off of my coat and grabbed the auric by his tricep.

"Let's go," I growled, "Blues will be here any minute."

As if on cue, distant sirens began to screech across the city. I could hear footsteps begin to shuffle upstairs, along with a few grunts and groans. SFPD would have a hell of a time containing an open building full of ragers, but it was no longer my problem.

Still in shock, the auric gave little protest as I pulled him out of the dispensary and into the night. The city street looked like a warzone, with rubble and bits of car strewn about everywhere. Half of the sedan I had aimed for was on its side, charred almost to ash and pressed up against the opposing building. The other half was smoking on top of an adjacent truck, which wasn't in much better shape.

I dragged the auric past the debris, feeling the street shiver like an aftershock as the surrounding buildings readjusted to their foundations. The blast had undoubtedly drawn the attention of the few workers and street people in the alley, and the area would be buzzing with activity in no time. I ducked into the cul-de-sac and entered a passcode on my digitab. My cruiser came to life as we approached, and I pushed a button on its side compartment to release it and grab a few emergency supplies.

"Hold still," I said to the auric, placing one hand on the back of his neck and driving a syringe into his jawbone.

"Mother pisser!" he cursed thickly, squirming out from my grip. "The hell was that?"

"Oxadrenalthaline," I said, pricking my forehead with a smaller needle. A soothing warmth pulsed through the side of my face as the medicine took effect, masking the pain receptors in my temple. "Temporary, but should negate the swelling."

I threw the empty syringes back in the compartment and straddled the cruiser, nodding at the small passenger seat behind me. "Get on."

The auric looked at me incredulously, massaging his jaw. In the stronger light of the street his angular features stood out more prominently, high cheekbones and a strong nose under slightly almond-shaped eyes. He had an almost elvish look to him, with olive-tinted skin and ears that stuck out acutely under shaggy brown hair.

"You've got to be kidding me," he said, poking at his tongue. "You almost killed me. Why'd I go anywhere with you?"

I sighed, tapping a button on my digitab and allowing my lenses to synchronize with the auric's features in the dim light. Records from the NIGHT database began popping up in the display, replete with pictures of the auric at various ages and silent holovids of him from security footage.

"Tribe Achebe, born twenty-one November, twenty forty-three in Troy, Michigan," I began, reading off the police reports. "Two charges of robbery and one charge unauthorized Oxidium possession in Detroit by the age of fourteen, three days in the VPen. Moved to San Francisco in twenty fifty-nine. Since then, three charges of breaking-and-entering, two Oxidium charges, revolutionary affiliations, and it looks like you're behind on your rent."

The thief looked at me blankly, rubbing his face.

"Should I continue?" I said.

He shrugged, his ear and nose piercings jingling. "Nothing the police don't already know."

"I also put a tracer on your neck, so there's that."

The auric reached a hand back to probe at the device I had placed while applying the syringe. He squinted at me irritably.

"Try to remove it and it will stick you with a neurotoxin," I continued. "I'll be happy to find a VPen for you when you wake up."

He looked at me for another heartbeat, then shrugged again and got on the cruiser. I wheeled it around and took it out of the cul-de-sac, charting a route out of the alleyway and towards the Columbus-Farrow storefronts, a figurative stone's throw from the NIGHT headquarters.

When the aurics started multiplying and threatening local census percentages with their population numbers, public opinion quickly changed from what bordered on novelty and casual ignorance to fear and outrage. The first generation, though of humans, was not human, but could be tolerated as a sort of guilty by-product of ceridium research. The second generation, which began to gain some momentum as their numbers and support grew towards establishing their own communities, could not be afforded the same magnanimity. By the time the third generation of the so-called "underraces," or even more pejoratively, "nonhumans," came of adulthood, they would have a full-scale civil war threatening to bloody their hands.

The governments of most nations responded to the rising populations and unrest in similar clichéd fashions. Several European, African, and South American countries saw the opportunity for assimilation and immediately amended their legal codes to provide space for the new underrace communities. A handful of smaller nations, unequipped to deal with the new generations of tusked, horned, or pointy-eared people in their midst tried to squash any type of resistance with military might, and were wholly unprepared for the result. Laos, Moldova, and Côte d'Ivoire were now underrace territories. Ecuador, Estonia, and the Dominican Republic belonged to the revolutionaries. The underraces had claimed Iceland for themselves, and the majority of North America and western Europe had their hands full with trying to keep a lid on revolutionary dissent. Thog'run II, their self-appointed king, built his Northern California capital on the backs of his enemies and gave the newer races a title and a purpose: aurics, a people who were meant to rule over others, and worthy of the gold of their namesake.

Most countries with the political and military might to support it quickly developed a security organization to deal with this new threat, or hired a third party to do it for them. The United States spared neither expense nor time in creating the National Intelligence Guard of Human Technology, a paramilitary force built exclusively to identify and protect against the influx of people that the nation's cities could not handle, and for which its fragile sense of ethnic identity could not make room. The American public at large, exhausted from years at war abroad, was only too happy to focus its military paranoia within.

The Pacific South NIGHT headquarters were strategically located on the island of Alcatraz, a choice which I had begun to find more and more fitting. It was stolen land from the Native Americans that had been turned into lighthouse, then prison, then tourist attraction, and now a bastion of humanity against a rising tide of underraces that humans had created but didn't understand. A new lighthouse of sorts that was only accessible by water or air, with a good deal of the country's internal defense budget behind it. The facility's lower levels housed approximately two hundred NIGHT foot soldiers, officials, Daypaths, Nightpaths, and Inquisitors, with room for over fifty virtual penitentiary inhabitants. It was rivaled in size only by the Atlantic North headquarters on the reclaimed Liberty Island in New York.

I sped through the side streets adjacent to Old Market, taking advantage of the quiet midnight roads. I pulled up a number on my cruiser console and clicked it to connect.

"Nightpath," Striker's voice grated in my ear. "What the hell just happened?"

"Patch me into Karthax, Striker," I replied.

"Karthax is in Cuba, hombre," he said, a bit too lazily for my liking.

"*Now*, Striker," I yelled into the air in front of me. The auric behind me shifted uncomfortably as we accelerated around a corner.

"Piss off, Nightpath," Striker retorted, but the console clicked with a temporary display, asking me politely to hold.

"Yeah?" a sleepy voice spoke into my earpiece after a moment.

"Madge, is that you?" I said. "We have a situation here-"

"Do you know what time it is here, Eskander?"

"Are you sleeping?!"

"Quarter to three. AM. *In the morning*." She sounded exhausted. Doubling up as a Daypath and the Inquisitor General's personal security would do that to you.

"Just put Karthax on, will you?" I asked as politely as I could muster.

"Alright," she said with a yawn.

I turned another corner, crossing Old Market and heading north for the Columbus-Farrow storefronts.

The earpiece clicked again as Madge authorized my call. After a few seconds, I could hear the muted sound of a conversation in the background.

"Karthax," a gravelly voice said.

"Inquisitor General," I acknowledged, launching into my report. "Our intel on the rigged storefronts may be compromised. Times and disarm code were both incorrect, and the location was full of ragers. I suspect the same of North Beach, and am headed there now."

There was a brief silence on the call, broken only by the distant din of voices. I checked the upper level of traffic and engaged the cruiser's boosters.

"That won't be necessary," Karthax's voice came back on the line. "Return to headquarters for debriefing."

"Sir?" I asked incredulously. "I'm five away from Columbus-Farrow, and if our intel on them is wrong as well-"

"Return to headquarters," he said again, this time with authority. "That will do, Nightpath." The console clicked. I punched the cruiser's handlebar in frustration.

"That guy sounds like an ass," the auric remarked from behind me.

"You could hear him?" I asked.

"I didn't need to," he said.

The Inquisitor General's words didn't sit well with me. Karthax, normally laconic by any standard, would still have more to say about a botched job. That he didn't have further instructions for me or at least some vocal interest in my well-being made me a little nervous.

On a whim, I wheeled the cruiser off of the main road and down a one-way street to approach Columbus-Farrow from a less obvious direction. Something akin to intuition snaked its way uncomfortably around my torso and settled in the pit of my stomach, and I was suddenly paranoid about coming into contact with any other NIGHTs heading to the North Beach storefronts. I gunned the engine and flew through several intersections, buildings and floating streetlights blurring by me.

"Where are we going, man?" the auric complained. "I told you, I didn't do anything."

"What do you know about the ragers at the Oxidium dispensary?" I asked him over my shoulder.

"Are you my lawyer?" he objected. "I don't have to tell you anything."

"You've got one estranged sister in Queens who works as a security guard," I said, reading off the police reports from the corner of my eye, "and two brothers who might as well be revolutionaries. Your probation is up in four months, but any other incidents will put you straight back into the VPen, for two weeks this time. Your most recent mailing address-"

"Alright, alright!" he relented. "Nothing much. It's...it was just a safehouse. The store was on the bottom, and a shelter on top. The owners sold Ox to friends of the cause, and funneled it back behind the scenes to keep the ragers calm and fed. Hiding in plain sight, you know how it is."

"You're a good Samaritan, then?" I had a hard time believing the thief had a philanthropic streak, but people can surprise you.

"Something like that," he said. "People need those drugs, man."

He wasn't wrong. The Oxidium, which was initially marketed as a prescription against the effects of ceridium exposure, turned out to be a double-edged weapon against its intended consumers. For humans, it had the addictive tendencies of a narcotic with performance enhancers. For those with the auric gene, it had the same qualities, but with the unintended benefit of combating the rage plague that had begun to appear in the second generation of underraces.

Its addictive dependency had proven to outweigh its usefulness, however. Over time, auric exposure to Oxidium usually still resulted in the user devolving into a particular kind of psychosis that could be set off by the slightest provocation, bolstered by Oxidium-induced strength and reflexes. The rage plague's root cause eluded even the most erudite of government scientists, and its symptoms could only be mitigated, albeit temporarily, by Oxidium.

"What do you know about these two buildings?" I asked the auric, pointing at the North Beach locations on the console.

He shifted to peer over my shoulder, reading the map as I slowed the cruiser and doubled back to circle the storefronts.

"Nothing, man. Those aren't ours," Tribe said. "They're run by the auric king's people. You'll have to ask him."

"I'll be sure to do that when I meet him," I quipped.

As we turned on Columbus-Farrow, the lights and sounds increased exponentially, with augmented reality digital ads of local bars and strip clubs filling my vision like carnivalesque holograms. Small, carefully manicured trees sat at intervals along the sidewalks, the only semblance of nature in the neon and concrete neighborhood.

We didn't get very far. Dozens of clubbers and pub crawlers milled about in the middle of the street, being ushered away from a hastily set up perimeter around one of the storefronts in question. A thin line of yellow police tape cordoned off half of the block, and SFPD officers directed traffic and spoke with passersby. Two NIGHT vehicles sat placidly on the sidewalk on the opposite side of the block behind the police tape, riderless.

My cruiser's console beeped with an incoming call from Striker. I ignored it, lowering the bike onto the ground level and maneuvering in between the pedestrians and stopped cars towards the perimeter.

I brought the vehicle to a halt just outside of the yellow tape and swung my leg over the side. Tribe started to get off as well, but I put a hand firmly on his chest.

"Stay here," I said, pushing him back onto the bike. His tanned face scrunched in protest, but he sat still.

I walked a few paces towards a couple of police officers standing on the sidewalk, and turned back towards the cruiser. Catching Tribe's eye, I tapped pointedly at the back of my neck, and then at him. He understood my meaning, morosely rooting himself to the cruiser.

The Blues straightened perceptibly as they saw me approach. There was no love lost between the city's peacekeeping force and the government's pet defense agency, but SFPD had neither the technology nor the mancy training to back up anything more than hollow protests about NIGHT jurisdiction over their crime scenes. To them, interacting with us was a little bit like being forced to do a group project with the school bully.

"Evening, officers," I said, trying to put them at ease. "What's the scene look like here?"

"Under control," one of them, a short Caucasian fellow with a close-cropped beard, replied gruffly. The other, a stocky African American woman, just stared at me.

"Bomb threat, taken care of," he continued, eyeing my torn clothing and dirty brown hair, which must have been darker than usual with dust and who knew what else.

I nodded, looking at the building behind the police tape. "Have you evacuated? Any inhabitants?"

"Not that we know of," he said tersely.

I scanned the storefront for a few more moments, wondering who among the other NIGHTs had been sent to investigate it and what they had found. I suspected that the other North Beach building was similarly under control, and it made me shiver. I didn't care for the idea that the downtown dispensary was special, or that someone knew when I would be there, and why. It made me feel like an open target.

"Any drones catch anything?" I asked at length.

"Aren't any drones left around here," the man said.

I nodded again, expecting as much. "Carry on." I turned on my heel, walking back towards the cruiser.

"I hate them," I heard the woman say when she thought I was out of earshot.

My earpiece buzzed twice as I walked over, alerting me of two waiting messages. Tribe had moved into the driver's seat and was holding up a small digitab and fiddling with the console. The device finished syncing as I reached the cruiser, enabling the vehicle's sound system and beginning to play a turn-of-the-century reggae anthem.

The auric looked up as I approached, grinning. "I've never sat in one of these before!" he exclaimed.

"Why do I not believe you?" I muttered under my breath, waving a hand and killing the sound system. He jumped back into the passenger seat and I straddled the cruiser, enabling the messages on my lens display. The bike lurched forward under my touch as we turned away from the perimeter.

Both messages were sent within twenty seconds of each other. The first, from Striker, read simply: *Return to HQ.* The second, barely more informative, was from Madge.

HQ not safe, it read. *Disappear.*

I allowed the messages to fade from my display, letting the bike cruise for a few blocks. Until thirty minutes ago, my occupation had been fairly straightforward: root out enemies of the state, neutralize or otherwise eliminate them, and generally keep myself out of harm's way while doing it. I'm ordinarily very good at my job, but in the past half hour, things had become infinitely more complicated. The network of NIGHT informants was normally airtight, and I had never been given a reason to doubt my intel. For things to have gone south so quickly was a huge warning sign, never mind Madge's message, which I trusted implicitly.

The night wind ruffled my hair as I drove us along aimlessly, considering. I needed time and I needed information, and didn't know how to find either. As much as I hated to admit it, I needed help.

"We're going to take a detour," I said to the auric behind me.

"Whatever man, I don't have any place to be," he replied lazily.

Taking a deep breath, I used the cruiser console to disengage the bike and my digitab from the network, leaving me technologically blind against anything that was happening in the digital sphere, but protecting us from being traced.

"Know anyone that can hack into a mainframe?" I asked Tribe.

"No," he said thoughtfully from behind me, "but I bet I know someone who does."

THREE

Baseball is the best human sport in existence. After soccer. Soccer is the best human sport in existence.

-The Sigil of Sparks

It took a lot longer to reach Tribe's contact without the cruiser's network-enabled routefinder, but as soon as we pulled into the Richmond district I had a fair idea of whom he was taking me to see. Paradoxically, there were very few fences who worked this far out from the city center and close to the Golden Gate. Only a small number of people had sway with the auric king's outpost beneath the erstwhile Presidio less than a mile away.

Alina Hadzic was a former big leaguer and relief pitcher, leading the San Francisco Giants to three Global Championships and two World Series, headlining the papers as the first half-auric woman to play in the majors. A rookie sensation, she skyrocketed to the top of the player rankings for her first decade of play, retiring early to serve in the Fourth Gulf War and returning with a well-documented interest in visiting the underrace capital north of the city, Aurichome. Rather than making the rounds as a politician or sports commentator, as seemed to have become the standard pipeline for retired athletes, she quietly opened a sports-themed bar on the outskirts of the Richmond.

It was no secret that after Hadzic returned from overseas, she had developed more than a little vocal sympathy for the auric king and his revolutionary cause. Call it PTSD, going native, or whatever, but she isolated what small celebrity platform she had made for herself by making a few choice comments about the American government and its lack of institutional support for the underraces.

It was, however, much less known that her bar was an underground railroad for rev movement. Most underrace citizens with their pointed ears to the ground knew about her operation, and that hers was a safe place for revolutionaries. Among their own, they called her the Pitcher.

We pulled up in front of the sports bar, a large space that was all windows, stuck between two towering, hastily constructed apartment buildings. Flags from various Bay Area sports teams stuck out colorfully from an orange- and black-painted awning. A small, AR-enabled sign hung over the heavy front door, flashing *They Might Be Giant* in three-dimensional curvilinear script. The place looked closed for the night and empty, dark except for a few small lights within.

My temple had started throbbing during our ride as the Oxadrenalthaline wore off. I rubbed at it gently as I parked the cruiser, reaching into the side compartment for another syringe.

"You want one?" I asked the auric, who had hopped off the bike and was making his way to a tiny corridor on the left side of the building.

"Nah," he drawled, his mouth visibly swollen, "she'll take care of it."

I pricked my temple and felt my vision clear immediately. Scanning the street for any movement and seeing none, I followed the thief into the alleyway.

He was already tapping away furiously at his digitab, pressing it up against a mechanism on the building's side entrance. The lock quietly beeped, and Tribe pushed the door open with a palm. He flashed me a toothy, blood-stained grin, and stepped inside.

Roughly two seconds later, he came hurtling back out of the door, slamming into the wall of the adjacent building and falling into a heap on the ground. My hand shot to the pistol within my coat, but before I could move, a shadow leapt through the side entrance and on top of the hapless auric, growling and tearing at his jacket.

"*Down*, Buster!" a voice called from within the bar. A woman stuck her head out into the alley, her frizzy hair looking like an angry octopus in the darkness.

"Tribe, that you?" she said, reaching out a hand to tug on the wolf's scruff. The hound reluctantly responded to her touch, easing off of Tribe and sitting at the woman's feet.

The woman stepped into the alleyway, helping Tribe to his feet. "The hell, man? How many times do I have to tell you to let me know when you're coming?"

"Sorry," the auric said, dusting himself off. "When's he going to stop doing that?"

I stood unnoticed, watching the exchange. The woman cut a slender but muscular figure in the gloom, her strong arms exposed under a faded black jersey.

I cleared my throat awkwardly. "Nice to see you, Alina."

The Pitcher looked up at me, startled, then nodded. "Nightpath."

She turned back to Tribe and ushered him into the building. "What did you do to your face?"

The auric stuck a thumb out in my direction as he ducked inside. Alina glowered at me again and then down at the wolf, who was waiting patiently.

"Great guard dog you are," she said spitefully.

He wagged his tail happily in response. I've always been good with dogs.

I followed the half-auric and her wolf companion into the room, a small service area with neatly stacked plates, tankards, and silverware. She closed the door behind us and led me into the sports bar proper, a sprawling, open space with several wooden tables and chairs positioned strategically around augmented reality display monitors. An L-shaped bar hugged the far corner of the room, wiped impeccably clean and gleaming under a few overhead lights. I marveled at the wall space, which was crowded with memorabilia, signed jerseys, and team flags.

"Nice place," I said stupidly.

The Pitcher ignored me and ushered Tribe to the bar, stepping behind it to grab a couple of glasses. The wolf wandered into a spot near a small standing fan and plopped himself down, licking himself contentedly.

"Rum and coke?" Alina asked the auric, rummaging behind the counter.

"Please," he said, picking at his jaw.

"Nightpath?" her muffled voice echoed from behind the bar.

"Double scotch, no ice," I called back to her, reading an inscription on a signed photo of Alina posing in her Giants uniform with the previous city mayor. *To Alina*, it read, *for giving all of us an example to follow*. I wondered what he thought of her now that she was on the other side of the political fence.

The half-auric reappeared behind the bar, expertly mixing a drink for each of us. I walked over and sat down at one of the cushioned stools, grabbing a handful of mixed pretzels and nuts, suddenly starving. Tribe gingerly lifted his drink to his mouth, trying to figure out how to drink it around his swollen tongue.

"I didn't realize how badly you were hurt," she said, eyeing me accusingly.

I put my hand up in resignation and took a sip of the scotch, following it with some of the pretzels. The mix of peat and salt tasted incredible, and I could feel my body relax a bit.

"Here," Alina said, taking the drink from Tribe's hand and reaching behind the bar again. She pulled out a pure ceridium crystal, dropping it into an empty glass and grinding it into dust with a spoon. Emptying the cup's contents into a calloused palm, she spoke several words in an earthy language that sounded like autumn leaves rustling. She cupped Tribe's chin in her free hand, drizzling the dust over his jaw and face.

The auric's normally swarthy visage pulsed with an azure light as the magic took effect. The glow subsided after several seconds, but his face retained a youthful, rested look to it.

"Thanks," he said, throwing back his drink.

Alina glanced at my forehead, pointing. "You want me to look at that?"

"I'll be alright," I said, then raised an eyebrow at her wryly. "Pitcher, barkeep, *and* terramancer?"

"What, I can't have a hobby?"

I raised my hands again in submission, but made a mental note to do some research about where she learned magic, and from whom.

"What's the sitch?" she said abruptly, changing the subject. "It's not often that I get one A.M. visits from government turncoats."

I ignored the barb and took another sip of scotch. "Someone tried to kill me," I said plainly.

"You'll have to be more specific."

I related the story of the evening's events, leaving out the specifics of my mission briefing but revealing enough information to let her know my suspicions of the faulty intel and my reluctance to return to the NIGHT headquarters. I finished by explaining how the North Beach jobs went off without a hitch, and that I was off the grid because of Madge's warning.

The half-auric took it all in silently, sipping a clear liquid through a straw. When I completed my story, she looked off in the distance for a few minutes, thinking. I waited patiently, swirling the glass in my hand and trying not to stare at her. Even in the bar light, her brown mane shimmered, tumbling down her strong shoulders and framing her pale face. The tips of her softly pointed ears peeked out beneath the nest of curls, and a splash of freckles across her small nose made her face look a little playful.

I coughed politely and busied myself looking at the wall decorations. Tribe went around the bar and started mixing himself another drink, and Buster snored softly nearby, having put himself to sleep.

"What do you want from me?" Alina asked finally, turning her piercing blue eyes on me.

I motioned towards Tribe. "This one thinks you can help me find someone who can hack into the NIGHT HQ's mainframe."

"How is that going to help?"

I took another swig of scotch. "I'm a hundred percent certain tonight wasn't supposed to go down the way it did, and about seventy percent sure it was an inside job." My mouth burned a little from the alcohol, but I could feel my body warm to it comfortingly. "The place was supposed to have been deserted, with a minor incendiary that should have gone off thirteen minutes later."

The Pitcher nodded, sipping softly at her drink.

"My supplied passcode was incorrect," I continued, "and that bomb could have taken out a whole block without the shadow shield attached to it. Whoever set up the job either didn't know about the ragers or didn't care about killing all of them, and the whole street with them."

I finished off the scotch, popping a few more pretzels in my mouth. "More importantly, they knew when I was going to be there, and made every effort to make sure I was caught in that blast. It's only because of the thief," I pointed at Tribe again, "that we all made it out of there alive."

The auric, who had been listening absently, perked up at that, saluting me ridiculously with his drink.

"There are only two groups who would have access to my mission intel. Any of the revolutionary informants' lives would be forfeit if they provided false information. The NIGHTs would either give them up to the auric king for his own judgment on their betrayal, or otherwise have them taken care of."

I set down the glass quietly, allowing the information to sink in.

"That leaves-"

"The NIGHTs themselves," Alina finished my sentence.

I nodded, sitting back in the stool and crossing my arms.

"Piss," Tribe said perfunctorily.

"So," I said, "I need someone who can hack into the NIGHT mainframe and get me more information about the botched briefing. I have my lens recording of the whole thing, and audio of my conversation with Striker, but he's a cog in the machine. I have a pretty good idea of who sent the order, but I need proof before I can take it national."

The Pitcher sat in thought, twirling her finger through an unruly curl. It was almost rust-colored in the soft light.

"Gloric Vunderfel," she said eventually.

"Is that a name?"

Alina nodded.

"Never heard of him," I complained.

"Why would you?" she retorted.

"The technomancer!" Tribe chimed in.

I felt my brow furrow in confusion. "Technomancy? Is that a thing?"

Both of them looked at me as though I had asked if the earth really does go around the sun. I'm not used to being uninformed.

"How do we find him?" I asked, swallowing my pride.

"Easy," the Pitcher replied, reaching into a pocket for her digitab. "I've got him on speed dial."

Before she could use the device, Buster jumped up from his place in the corner, growling menacingly at the street. The three of us started, turning as one to face the large windows.

It was difficult to see out into the dark street outside, but I could make out ten or more shadowy figures, obscured in the night and approaching *They Might Be Giant*. Soft blue lights swayed as they moved, the only visible signs of their ceridium weapons.

"Down!" I yelled, trusting the others had seen the hit squad as well, or would at least listen to my command. I dove behind a nearby table and threw my body against it to uproot it in front of me. I could hear a crash of glasses behind me as Alina and Tribe flattened themselves against the bar.

The shadows opened fire on the sports bar. Silent ceridium bullets pelted through the establishment's windows like horizontal rain, making ugly sounds as they lodged into the tables and walls. Glass shattered as the projectiles hit tankards and framed pictures, and several cobalt bullets streaked by me and thudded into the heavy table.

I produced a capsule from my coat and unsheathed my pistol, feeling the adrenaline course through me and trying to remain calm. I waited for the silence that would follow the volley as they reloaded their weapons, but it didn't come. Through the cacophony of impact I could hear muffled sounds of glass breaking at the front of the building as several of the assailants burst through the windows under cover fire.

"Now!" I yelled, hoping the others could hear me.

I rolled out from behind the table, riding the adrenaline but not letting it take over my reflexes. I fired on instinct where I had previously heard movement, and my aim was true, taking an auric in the face with a ceridium bullet of my own. He spun backwards through the window and into the street. I continued my roll as a goblin-sized auric adjacent to the first fired at me. Dodging the projectile, I crushed the capsule and called out a word as I came into a crouch. I leveled my hand at the little man, sending a bolt of shadow towards him. It hit him in the chest, lifting him ass over teakettle through the window.

There was a brief reprieve as the cover fire squad exhausted their ammo and reloaded their weapons. I scrambled behind a metal case that held various trophies and awards, switching my pistol to my left hand and reaching for the hilt of my nightblade. I could hear glass crunching and wood scraping against the floor as the hit squad made their way into the room.

Alina slid from her position behind the bar, coming out of a windup and hurling a tankard end-over-end towards an advancing auric. The projectile hit him in the cheek like a wrecking ball, leaving him sprawling over a table. The assassin nearest to him fired on the Pitcher, but she spun like a dancer, feeding another glass from her left hand into her right. She came out of her turn and sent it towards him, but he lifted his gun in time to deflect it.

It didn't matter. A dark shape streaked towards him, fur and claws and death. Buster leapt from the hiding place he had stalked to, tearing at the auric mercilessly with his teeth and hind paws. I wouldn't have made it very far in my line of work being squeamish, but I still blanched a little at the sound.

Having reloaded, the hit squad opened fire again, forcing Alina to duck back behind the bar. I wondered where Tribe had gotten himself to, then heard faint chanting from the side of the room. I peeked around the cabinet, and could make out the telltale signs of a spell in the works. A little auric caster was moving his arms wildly, embers sparkling at his fingertips.

"Pyromancer!" I yelled a warning at my compatriots. A fire spell among the wooden furniture of the sports bar would have the effect of a grenade in a pile of kindling.

I needn't have worried. Tribe detached himself from the wall nearest to the caster, putting his hand on the gnome's mouth and cutting of the spell. The thief withdrew a knife from some hidden place on his body, thrusting it in between the pyromancer's neck and shoulder. The assassin convulsed as Tribe pulled away, melting back into the shadows.

I didn't have much time to consider my next move, as a loud crash came from the service area nearby. I had completely forgotten about the side entrance, and almost paid for it with my life. I turned around just as a hulking auric shouldered his way into the main bar area, taking most of the wall with him and collapsing the room into rubble as he came around the service area's small doorway. He noticed me immediately, swiping a giant hand at my face.

I dropped to the floor, feeling the fist fly over my head and crunch into the metal cabinet behind me. I dove between the troll's legs and turned, drawing the nightblade out in front of me. The sword extended as it cleared the little sheath, ratcheting into place with a hum into its full size. A thin line of ceridium ran the length of the slightly curved blade, glowing faintly in the darkness.

The auric was more nimble than he had any right to be, backing out of the way of my draw and parrying it with a dagger the size of a baseball bat. He lashed at me again with his free hand, and I sidestepped out of his reach, being careful to keep his massive form in between myself and the firefight. I could see the others out of the corner of my eye, engaging more assassins coming through the windows.

I leveled my pistol at the troll and fired from point blank range, but he swept the long dagger in front of his body as I pulled the trigger, knocking the weapon from my hand and spoiling my shot. I let the pistol fall and gripped my nightblade's hilt with two hands, driving it towards his sizeable midsection. The motion was too quick for the brute to parry, and he smacked at the blade with his bare hand, slicing off two fingers the size of sausages. He grunted but advanced towards me, swinging his horned head and slashing wildly with his dirk. I moved to catch the dagger on my nightblade, then shifted my weight to bring the sword in a diagonal slash. The troll's arm and dagger fell to the floor.

He howled but leapt towards me, adrenaline and Oxidium lending him a partial immunity to the pain. He hooked at me with a three-fingered hand, punching me in the ear painfully. I moved with the strike to lessen the impact, using the momentum to spin away from him. I reversed the grip on my nightblade, thrusting it behind me and into his heart. Feeling his dead weight catch on the blade, I pulled it away and let the troll fall.

I turned back towards the front of the bar, and a nightmare sprang through one of the broken windows. Tribe, Alina, and the wolf were still fending off the attackers, oblivious to the peril that pursued them. I tried to call out, but an unfamiliar sensation stayed my tongue.

He was in most ways nondescript, an average auric with skin the color of ash. His short hair was cut close to his round head, accentuating the thin white ears protruding from his skull. Even his piglike snout and tusks were small, almost disappearing against his pale complexion as if uncomfortable with drawing any attention. The only thing remarkable about him was his burgundy leather coat, which gleamed like blood in the low light.

Yet, something about him was unusual, in the way he confidently strode into the bar with single-minded purpose, a hunter unerringly stalking his prey. I could see his eyes glowing crimson in the darkness, and recognized the emotion that had frozen me.

Fear.

He looked in my direction, and nodded once in salute. Then he did the strangest thing I have seen before or since.

The auric put two fingers out to his side, slicing them through the air in an oval shape. With his other hand, he threw a handful of what looked like seeds on the ground in front of him, letting out a sharp, barking whistle through his tusked mouth.

The result was catastrophic. A gash opened in the air where the seeds had fallen, a tear in the fabric of the universe. From within, a roar could be heard, and the building rumbled in response. The crack widened, and an orange fire began to spill forth.

The auric whistled again, and his underlings immediately disengaged to evacuate. Without another glance, he glided out of the room as smoothly as he had come, disappearing into the night.

The motion was enough to spur me into action. I flicked the nightblade free of blood, scooped up my discarded pistol and sheathed my weapons as I ran over to the others, who were standing bewildered at the attackers' sudden retreat and the new threat. Bolts of ochre fire began fizzing out of the tear into the room, instantly setting the wooden furniture ablaze.

"We've got to get out of here!" I shouted to Alina, trying to shake her from shock. "Is there another exit?"

She looked at me, then at the rubble in front of the side room. Blinking a couple of times, she nodded dumbly, moving towards the back of the room.

A blistering heat began to build from the front of the bar, and I put myself in between it and Tribe as we followed the half-auric. Buster bounded in front of us, knowing the way. Fire arrows continued to sting the room, pelting at the back of my coat. Alina took us to a storage area, dragging away a couple of empty kegs stacked on top of one another.

I could feel the temperature rising as the building burned. Smoke began to fill the room as the place caught on fire, and it took all of my patience not to scream at Alina to hurry it up. She fidgeted with a latch halfway up the wall, opening a hidden door into a small passageway. The wolf immediately jumped through it, followed by Tribe and Alina. I came through it last, hearing one of the building's rafters collapse behind me.

The night air was like a splash of cold water on my burning lungs. I breathed deeply, hacking the smoke out of my body. I looked around, noticing that the alley was actually just a tiny yard protected on all sides by the adjoining structures. Alina was already unlocking a small gate that led in between two of the buildings, next to invisible from the street. We rushed through the passage in single file, stopping briefly to make sure no one was lying in wait for us outside.

Convinced that the coast was clear, we filtered out into the street, catching our breath and hearing the sounds of destruction from *They Might Be Giant*'s direction. The night was quiet in comparison to the burning building, and I stood with my hand on my knees for a few moments, my lungs still on fire and my heart pulsing in my chest. Tribe coughed his way over to a nearby SUV, using his digitab to disable the security systems. He engaged the engine and opened the passenger doors with a button, beckoning towards us.

"Come on, we've got to go before everything else falls apart," he called from the driver's seat.

I couldn't disagree. I gently pushed Alina forward, noticing silent tears running down her soot-stained cheeks. She joined Tribe in the cab of the black truck, and I jumped into the back with Buster. Closing the doors, the auric gunned the accelerator and took us away from the Richmond.

Through the SUV's insulated windows, I could hear muted police sirens begin to wail into the night.

FOUR

We are one race, one people, one family. From today until the end of eternity, we now have one home.

> -Thog'run II, King of Aurichome

The faintest grey light of dawn was just beginning to stain the horizon by the time we made it to the outskirts of Gloric's neighborhood in Santa Clara. The highway had been relatively quiet after we had passed through San Francisco's southern borders, picking up again slightly as we reached the fringes of the technological center of the world. I fought to stay awake as my normal bedtime came and went, the SUV's ergonomically cushioned seats comfortably embracing my exhausted body.

The others had kept to themselves for most of the drive, as tired as I was and less in practice at being shot at. Alina sat staring out of the tinted windows as the city rolled past us, coming out of her shock only to heal my injuries and scratch at Buster distractedly. Tribe, for once, held onto his own thoughts, driving the speed limit and keeping to the lower level of traffic to avoid drawing unnecessary attention upon us. The silence was broken only by the sounds of the road and Tribe's retro hip hop music, softly playing through the truck's sound system.

I forced myself to remain alert, focusing on our current plan of action. If Tribe and Alina were correct in their assessment of Gloric Vunderfel's abilities, the hacker would be able to gain access to the NIGHT database and trace any communications that would have happened before my mission briefing. If we could establish any inconsistencies between the intel our informants had provided and that which was given to me, we could put together some sort of proof to clear my name. Tribe's fate would depend on the quality of evidence we were able to conjure, and so would Alina's, as the auric and half-auric were both now undoubtedly on whatever hit list I had the honor of headlining. At best, they would be incorrectly assumed to be co-conspirators in my continued well-being. At worst, they would be thought of as collateral damage.

My lens recording would be key in putting together a believable case towards my ignorance of the downtown storefront's true setup. Whoever was behind the faulty intel wanted me to die in that dispensary, and didn't mind the waste of life represented by blowing up fifty or more ragers. Finding the task to be more difficult than they anticipated, they somehow tracked me to *They Might Be Giant*, putting Tribe and Alina under the searchlight as well. I wouldn't be surprised if they were trying to put a bead out on Buster, too.

The more my exhausted mind ran through the scenarios, the less answers it came up with. None of the night's events made sense. I had already ruled out revolutionary involvement on the informants' part, trusting that the auric king had enough sway over his people to have instilled the fear of dragons in any potential defectors. That left only the NIGHT higher-ups with the kind of clearance to tinker with mission information like the bomb's timer, access codes, and the presence of innocents in the dispensary.

The composition and skillset of the hit squad sent after us would corroborate this theory. The presence of auric assassins would ordinarily suggest revolutionary involvement, but I couldn't think of what Aurichome had to gain by killing their own people in the dispensary, or by my death. More tellingly, the assassins' training and coordination was of a different stripe altogether. It was too organized, too similar to my own for the hit squad to have been solely the auric king's lot. The lead assassin in particular, for all his indistinctiveness, was unlike any auric I had seen.

The image of the mancer was like a spectre burned into my vision, his pale hands moving strangely and eyes burning with an evil light. I had no idea who he was or what kind of magic he had used against us, and that worried me. He exhibited neither the shadow arts training of a Nightpath, nor the life-affirming photomancy of a Daypath, nor the destructive and mind-controlling powers of an Inquisitor, placing him outside the traditional NIGHT magic education. My lenses had picked up no information on him whatsoever in their local database, not even a name or base personal record. Nothing. He might as well have been a ghost.

More importantly, I didn't know what was his stake in my death or for whom he was working. If it was indeed an inside operation by the NIGHT leadership, there were only a few people who could hold that sway, rigging an entire elite mission and hiring an unknown assassin when it went haywire. Karthax was the easy answer, but the Inquisitor General's potential motive was impenetrable to me. The man had been in charge of the Pacific South NIGHT headquarters for over a decade, with jurisdiction over Pacific North and Central Mountain as well. I couldn't think of a single reason why he'd want me dead, and a building full of ragers with me.

"The hell?" Tribe's voice came floating back from the cab, waking me from my reverie. I had dozed off despite myself, lulled by the long ride. I opened my eyes, blinking against the weak sunlight coming through the thief's open window.

"I'm off the network," he said, holding his digitab outside of the window, as though that would solve his problem. "I can't get back on."

"We're getting close to Gloric's neighborhood," Alina explained distantly, still staring out her window. "He only lets in who he wants."

"Weren't you supposed to text him or something?" Tribe complained.

"He'll know we're coming."

"How do you figure?"

"Because he knows almost everything that happens within a fifty mile radius," the Pitcher said, giving Tribe a sidelong glance. She rolled her shoulders, stretching. "And because we have nowhere else to go."

I peered outside the SUV's long side window, noticing the large track houses and apartment buildings with simple printed signs and electric street lamps, still on at this early hour. Unlike San Francisco or its South Bay cousin, San Jose, Santa Clara looked much like it would have a hundred years ago, with only a few augmented reality digads popping up here and there at small local shops.

Tribe pulled us into a nondescript driveway adjacent to a squat suburban house, ancient by modern standards. It was painted a pleasant color of peach, with a little garden in the front and a small picket fence bordering the sidewalk. It looked to me less like a technomancer's unbreachable fortress and more like a quaint bed and breakfast, but I suppose my small city apartment wasn't much to look at, either.

I stretched as I got out of the SUV, feeling the past twenty-four hours weighing heavily on my body and mind. I was used to being in mortal danger, but not usually several times in one night.

I stopped Tribe as he walked past me, reaching out to snatch the tracer from his neck with my thumb and index finger. He jumped at my touch, grabbing at his collar and looking at me accusingly.

"Neurotoxin!" he protested.

"Not really," I said evenly, disabling the little gadget and dropping it into a pocket. "Would you have stayed put if I told you otherwise?"

The thief stared at me for a moment, his eyes narrowing suspiciously, then shrugged and harrumphed in acquiescence.

Alina led us down the side of the house and through a wooden fence into the building's backyard, which held a larger version of the front garden. All manner of fruits and vegetables were being grown in neat rows, alongside a number of different decorative flowers. The heady fragrance was a nice contrast to the interior of the SUV, which had smelled mostly like wet dog. I breathed deeply, invigorated by the garden's motley bouquet.

The Pitcher walked briskly over to a small stairwell leading under the back wall of the house, stopping in front of a large metal door that was conspicuous in contrast to the rest of the decor. She pulled out her digitab and synced it with the door's intercom system, waiting for the other side to pick up.

"Alina," a tinny voice spoke out of the digitab. "It took you four minutes and twenty-five seconds longer than traffic suggests to get here."

The Pitcher looked up to a small camera lodged in the corner of the doorframe. "We stopped to get a drink for him," she said, pointing at Tribe. The auric waved sweetly at the camera.

"Very well," the digitab said. "Come in."

The door unlocked and swung ajar. On a hunch, I enabled my lenses' nonvisible spectrum analysis, and could see a grid of beams criss-crossing the entryway. An alarm sounded ridiculously as we each entered the building, cataloging each of us as being armed and chiming for each registered weapon. I counted eleven beeps.

"Ignore that," the voice on the digitab offered. "Outdated system; next version will just kill intruders on sight."

We continued into the interior of the building, which was in every way the polar opposite of its exterior. Cold stone walls lined the entry corridor, lit only by working pieces of computer gear piled up on either side of the walkway. Machines whirred, beeped, and clicked, echoing through the building in a strangely soothing cacophony. The air was dusty but dry, smelling sharply of metal and plastic.

Alina took us deeper into the house, down a few levels and around a few turns. The hodgepodge of electronic products increased like a breadcrumb trail, leading us to a central room that I estimated to be two floors directly under the backyard garden. Over twenty display monitors lined the walls directly ahead of us, fanned out in a semicircle around a huge leather chair. Several different kinds of antiquated keyboards and other input devices littered a large metal desk in between the chair and monitors.

"Welcome, guests," the voice from the digitab called from behind the chair, still a little tinny. "Why do I only get a visit when you're in trouble?"

The chair swiveled around, revealing a tiny bespectacled auric sitting cross-legged on its vast brown cushion. Wisps of white hair and long, perky ears peeked out from under a faded Santa Clara 49ers cap, and a secondary single-eye display jutted out in front of his glasses. His simple t-shirt and jeans were old but neatly pressed, and his abnormally large, sandaled feet poked out from under his legs. A rounded Canterbury cross rested at the hollow of his throat, standing out against his ebony skin.

"Hey, Glory," Alina said as she moved to embrace him. I used my lenses to quickly scan for any information about the gnome, and came up again with nothing. I was beginning to doubt my local database, and made a mental note to search again for him and the assassin when I was back on the network.

Tribe also went over to give the technomancer a fist bump and exchange pleasantries. The gnome turned his attention towards me, cocking his head to the side like a parrot considering a treat.

"What brings you here, Nightpath?"

"Gloric Vunderfel," I began stiffly, clearing my throat. "My associates here tell me-"

"I'm just kidding," he interrupted me with a chuckle. "I know why you're here."

The gnome spun in his chair back towards the desk and monitors, tapping with one hand at a mechanical keyboard and with another at an augmented reality holodisplay. Scenes from the past evening began to pop up on random monitors, from closed circuit cameras outside of *They Might Be Giant* to my lenses' current view of the back of Gloric's chair.

"What?" I asked, bewildered. I moved to the table next to the gnome, watching footage of myself stalking through the dispensary. "How do you know..." I trailed off.

"Ha!" the little auric exclaimed excitedly, typing away. "You can know anything if you have the right tools!"

The technomancer brought up several records on screen, reading bits and pieces of them out loud as they flashed through the various displays. "Eskander Aradowsi, born Eskander Arabiyya-Ferdowsi in modern Kurdistan, twenty thirty-nine. Family immigrated to the Ukraine in twenty forty-two, then to the United States in twenty forty-seven after the troll uprising. Military schooled, enrolled in NIGHT through special placement at age sixteen. First Nightpath of-"

"OK, OK, I get it," I said uncomfortably.

"Sucks, doesn't it?" Tribe said pointedly. I gave him a helpless look in response.

Gloric clicked a few more buttons, bringing up frames of the NIGHT headquarters on Alcatraz, the Oxidium dispensary, *They Might Be Giant*, and the auric assassin. "Where shall we begin?"

I took a deep breath, then launched into my recounting of the botched mission, attack on the sports bar, and encounter with the hit squad. I omitted my suspicions of Karthax and the NIGHT leadership, explaining only that I needed to hack into the headquarters' database to fill out the parts of the story that I didn't have access to.

The gnome listened patiently, swiping through different records and footage as I talked. When I finished, he sat back in his large chair, lacing his hairy hands behind his large head. "So, as I understand it," he said at last, "you want to break into the NIGHT mainframe to gain access to their records, proving you were set up and that there was a conspiracy to kill you."

I nodded.

"You probably also want me to reconfigure your digitab so that they can no longer trace you."

I nodded again, a bit sheepishly.

He turned his attention back to the monitors, tiny fingers working furiously as he brought up and edited several lines of code.

It took less than a minute. My digitab beeped, and I took it out of my pocket to see a smiley face blinking on the display. My lenses re-initialized, connecting to the network under an alias that the technomancer had set up for me. Classified records and images popped up on several of the monitors and my lens display.

"It's done," Gloric said, cracking his knuckles.

I read through the records, trying to ignore the fact that the little gnome had undone some of the country's most impregnable security systems with a few clicks.

"They have indeed been trying to kill you," the technomancer continued, "but it seems like it's nothing personal."

I sifted through the information, a vague map of the conspiracy beginning to form in my mind. It coalesced into an ironic image of Karthax, hero of the Fourth Gulf War and Inquisitor General of the NIGHTs, steering the free world out of the underrace-filled darkness and into the light. Armed with the military and magical might of the country's strongest forces, he would need only cede to the lesser evil to complete his conquest in the name of a perceived greater good.

"He wants to start a war," I breathed.

Tribe shifted awkwardly, a little bored. "Can somebody please explain what you two are going on about?"

"Our good Nightpath is discovering that his bosses aren't exactly what they purport to be," Gloric said.

I looked through the mission notes from my briefing, putting the pieces together.

"Karthax wants to start a war," I explained. "The dispensary was a front to generate military support to take the fight to the revolutionaries in their own house. I was meant to be collateral damage, my death a catalyst."

It made a certain kind of sense. The political and public outrage at losing a NIGHT operative in an act of terrorism could easily spark the already uneasy racial tensions into an all-out civil war. The strategy would be particularly convincing if Karthax could show that the revolutionaries didn't care about killing their own people, which is where the ragers came into the picture. Thus encouraged, the NIGHT leadership and its factors in Washington would almost have to give the Inquisitor General the green light for an all-out assault on Aurichome. It was an unthinkable proposition, given the size of the auric king's forces and their proven tenacity in guerilla warfare, but Karthax had always been ambitious.

It was something to go on, but there were several pieces still missing. I decided to press Gloric for more.

"The revs would never put their own people to the sword, so how did Karthax's people get access to the dispensary or switch the intel?" I asked. "And who was the auric assassin following us?"

The gnome slid a different keyboard into his hand, still double-typing. A number of monitors lit up with images of Karthax in his military uniform and beret, with the assassin lurking behind him, sending a chill down my spine. I could pick out a few words here and there embedded in several lines of code on-screen.

"The first I can't tell you much about," Gloric said at last. "Something about Project Watershed, but the information is behind a wall in the NIGHT headquarters."

"I don't understand, Glory," Alina chimed in for the first time, her hand resting in between Buster's bushy ears. "I've seen you get through all kinds of firewalls."

"Not a firewall, my dear. A real wall!" the gnome said, waggling his fingers excitedly. "In many ways, the NIGHTs' best protection is their isolation. Just like their island fortress, they keep a small portion of their classified files behind a physical wall off of the network."

"Like a safe?" I asked.

"Could be. Could be a cardboard box." The technomancer shrugged. "The important thing is that it's off the network. It allows them to keep some secrets, even away from their own people."

I thought about it for a moment, spinning the different scenarios around in my mind. "And the assassin?"

The party turned their attention as one to the images of Karthax and the assassin, pixilated but still menacing.

"There's not much to tell," Gloric drawled. "Ex-Special Forces, Karthax's pet in the war. Now works for him in odd jobs the government doesn't need to know about."

"Name?"

"Which one? He's had quite a few." The gnome scrolled through a few screens of text. "The most recent one is Agrid the Destroyer."

Tribe snorted, his piercings jangling. "Chump."

I looked over at Alina, who was staring up at a short clip of the assassin unleashing the meteor spell in *They Might Be Giant*. She wrapped her arms around her slim torso, trying not to shudder.

"His magic," she said meekly, "what was it?"

The technomancer nodded, raising his eyebrows enthusiastically. "Entromancy. Very interesting application. Very interesting!"

"Entermancy?" Tribe asked.

"*Entro*mancy," Gloric clarified. "Uses the concept of entropy as its foundation."

A dumb silence met the gnome's explanation. He looked up at us from his chair, then shook his head in resignation.

"I am so alone," he said, tapping a button and bringing a dictionary entry onscreen.

"Entropy," he continued. "One. Physics definition. 'A thermodynamic quantity representing the unavailability of a system's thermal energy for conversion into mechanical work, often interpreted as the degree of disorder or randomness in the system.'"

I coughed moronically. My working knowledge of physics was not great.

The gnome sighed and continued. "Two. 'A lack of order or predictability, or gradual decline into disorder.'"

"So, the assassin uses randomness to make stuff happen?" Tribe asked slowly.

"Precisely!" Gloric clapped his dark hands, excited that someone was speaking his language. "He depends on the chaos of the universe to initiate a chain reaction that ripples through time and space to generate a desired outcome, in a kind of deterministic butterfly effect."

We looked at him blankly, our tenuous grip on his explanation quickly slipping.

The gnome sat back in his seat, throwing his hands up in frustration. "He makes weird motions, things go boom."

"Got it," I said weakly, speaking for the group.

"I didn't see him use any ceridium," Alina said.

Gloric nodded again eagerly. "Doesn't need to. He's playing with the very fabric of the universe. It's chaos!"

I stared at the image of Karthax and the Destroyer, considering the implications of Gloric's explanation. Ceridium was the axis upon which all magic revolved, the ingredient which made it all possible. People who knew the science better than I did could tell you how the chemistry actually worked, but I had read enough of the history in my shadowmancy training to carry a conversation on the topic.

When the first green researchers discovered ceridium in the twenties, they had barely any idea of its application outside the creation of a renewable energy source. In that respect, they couldn't have done better. It was clean, it was stable, and most importantly, it was manufacturable. The chemical reaction they had engineered was a Philosopher's Stone of sorts, giving them the ability to turn mostly inert ingredients into a simple blue plasma that now powered over a quarter of the world.

Corporations were the first to monetize it for the purposes of sustainable energy, but it was the loosely assembled grassroots organizations that began to find alternative uses for the element. There were tinfoil hat conspiracy theorists who posited that ceridium was a government-seeded product intended to control the masses, alongside occult groups that believed it represented the ouroborus of nature and science and deserving of worship. The truth was somewhere in between.

As the history would have it, ceridium was a naturally-occurring element that the human race had depleted sometime during the war-torn western Middle Ages. Its use had been well-documented in archaic texts on the arcane arts, mostly ignored in the modern age where technology and reason took precedence over magic and fancy. People had no use at the time for a renewable energy source, having no idea what a motor or fossil fuel would look like. They did have a purpose for what they called blue orichalcum, which powered their spells and magical warfare.

The historical connection between blue orichalcum and ceridium was the missing link between the myths and legends present in most modern societies and the cultural memory that knew that all of the books, films, video games, and virtual reality simulators created about magic couldn't *all* be pure fantasy. It also explained the reference in most every civilization of the presence of other sentient beings that had declined in the later Middle Ages and beginning of the Renaissance. Modern science had confirmed that the underrace gene was essentially present in humans, but required a catalyst - direct or ambient exposure to ceridium - to become an observable phenotype.

Most of the world was not ready for the implications of this discovery. It meant that the long-eared, tusked, horned, or pig-snouted aurics that had begun to be born were just as human as the humans who birthed them. And because of the vast population burst at the turn of the twenty-first century, there was no place to put them, save underground, where most of the poorer human communities had moved. The "underrace" moniker was created, and it stuck, mostly because of the implied double meaning of inferiority.

In the fifty or so years since ceridium's discovery, the racial makeup of the world had changed, and entire schools of magic developed, ranging from the life-affirming arts of terramancy and hydromancy to the destructive forces of pyromancy and necromancy. The NIGHTs had spearheaded the charge on institution-led mancy research and training, dividing their quickly growing organization into its enduring three divisions, themselves based on magical skillsets. Nightpaths and Daypaths, who gained their namesakes from the shadow and light from which their mancy originated, were necessarily subordinate to team-leading Inquisitors. The latter straddled the line of destruction and inquest to tremendous effect, being tasked with sniffing out the most elusive of anti-government activity, and devising strategies that would then be carried out by the former. Yet, each type of magic required the mancer's use of ceridium, which made the assassin's exception all the more worrying.

"Wait a minute," Alina said suddenly, shaking me from my musing. "If the

Nightpath's digitab was off the grid since leaving North Beach, how did the assassin track him to-" her voice cracked a little. "To my place?"

The technomancer clicked a few buttons, wiping the screens blank. "Hmm, has anyone synced with any of his instruments since then? A digitab, or network-enabled vehicle, perhaps?"

As one, the Pitcher and I swung our heads towards Tribe. I glowered, remembering him tinkering with my cruiser's music system at the North Beach storefront.

The auric looked to one side, then the other, then back at us. "My fault!" he said, raising a hand uncomfortably.

Gloric shook his head and grabbed another keyboard, tapping away. After a few moments, all of our digitabs beeped.

"Should be good now," he said. "And don't worry about us here. The best they can get is a trace on the outskirts of the neighborhood."

"Um, thanks," Tribe said.

I couldn't shake the feeling that there was more to the situation than Karthax's bloodlust against the underraces and the presence of an impossibly magical auric hitman. I vented my concerns at the gnome, frustrated.

"How do we figure out more, then?" I asked, feeling my tiredness fuel my temper. "About why the revs are suddenly willing to kill their own people? And this-" I waved a hand towards the empty monitors. "Project Watershed?"

If the technomancer picked up on any of my irritation, he didn't let on. "I can call the auric king if you'd like," he said coolly. Having seen what he could do, I didn't doubt his sincerity, but I also wasn't ready to pick sides just yet.

Sensing my reticence, he continued. "Or, you can go and ask Karthax himself. Or the Sigil!"

Tribe and Alina both looked at the gnome quizzically, and I felt a vain burst of pride for not being in the dark for once.

"How do we get to him?" I asked haughtily.

"Follow the missing drones," he said, referring to the devices that had been increasingly disappearing from the city over the past few months.

"Nevada?" Alina asked.

"Reno!" Gloric exclaimed, typing at one of his virtual keyboards.

"The Sigil is in *Reno*?!" I said incredulously. Nevada was underrace territory, loyal to Aurichome and fiercely defended. Any air or land travel was normally diverted around the entire state.

"Sparks, to be specific!" the gnome said again, bringing up a map of the region and an image of what looked like the inside of a rustic tavern.

"I've always wanted to go, but who has the time?" he clucked. "We'll need a guide, one that can take us where we need to go and negotiate with the revolutionaries."

He punched a button on a mechanical keyboard, and a masked figure appeared on one of the monitors, framed by a single name.

"You're kidding," I said, disbelieving.

"Nope! Owes me a favor, much like I owe our pretty Pitcher here," the little auric beamed at Alina, who smiled back faintly, tugging at Buster's silky coat. Gloric turned in his chair, stretching.

"Now, who's up for breakfast?" he said.

FIVE

Dwarves and trolls are the most physiologically recognizable archetypes of the aurics, but they are no less human than the others. What most see as genetic difference is solely morphological.

-The Sigil of Sparks

I awoke to the cozy warmth of the afternoon sun beaming through open blinds. Blinking through my confusion, I looked around the room, initializing my lens display and reorienting myself to my surroundings.

It took a few moments, but as the sleep escaped my body, I slowly recalled falling facedown onto a mattress in one of Gloric's aboveground rooms, having eaten a full meal and even more magnificently, taken a hot shower. My body ached from a dozen bruises and sleeping in the same position, head throbbing from the Oxadrenalthaline hangover. Alina sat in the corner of the room reading a digitab, a beer in her hand. Tribe had his shaggy head propped on Buster's body, both sleeping peacefully. It looked like they had made friendly with each other.

"Thought you'd sleep all day," the Pitcher said without lifting her eyes from her digitab.

I sat up on the mattress, pinching the bridge of my nose as my head swam. "You and me both," I replied.

I walked over to her, steadying myself on the wall and feeling the room right itself under my feet. She lifted the can in my direction, and I took a swig from it gratefully. It was strong but smooth, the bitterness and alcohol clearing my head a little.

I passed the beer back to her and sat down with a grunt. "You doing OK?" I asked bluntly, feeling unusually companionable towards her. Avoiding getting killed together would do that to you.

Alina looked up at me with piercingly blue eyes, unreadable. Her curly hair was pulled back under a baseball cap, tame for the moment. "Yes."

I could hear the pain in her voice, and felt responsible. "If I had known that they would send-"

"I'm a big girl," she interrupted me. "I knew the risks when I aligned myself with Aurichome."

I nodded. "Sure, but they were targeting me, not you."

"They would have come for me eventually." She sighed, looking away for a moment, then back at me. "It doesn't really matter, does it?"

I shook my head. "We'll fix it," I said weakly, awkwardly putting a hand on her shoulder.

She let her gaze fall for a moment, then looked at an old digital time display hanging on the wall.

"We should get moving," she said briskly, putting away her digitab and rising to her feet. "Gloric said we'll need to get to the *Lucky Snake* by sundown."

I nodded and got up with her, walking over to rouse Tribe and the wolf. The thief woke with a start.

"It was gone when I got there!" he sputtered, shaking in my grip. Buster darted out from under him, bemused.

"Easy, buddy," I said gently. "Time to go."

Tribe's brown eyes focused on me, and he grinned. "Lunch?"

We grabbed a bite to eat from Gloric's considerably stocked kitchen, then collected the gnome from his control room. There was a brief argument, quickly resolved, when I insisted on driving the SUV.

"It's *my* car," Alina stated.

"Really?" I stammered, confused. "I thought he-"

"Hotwired it? Yeah," Tribe said helpfully. "It *is* her car, though."

I relented, and the Pitcher and thief took the front seats, while Gloric, Buster and I crowded the back.

It would take us just under two hours to make it back through the city and over the bridge into Oakland. It was a circuitous route, but I had convinced the party to let me stop by a safe drop not far from my apartment to pick up some more supplies and a clean set of clothes.

I still had trouble believing that our guide, a wanted enemy of the state, could be found across the Bay, not ten miles as the crow flies from the NIGHT headquarters. It was mute testament to how much information the organization purported to have on file about the so-called terrorist revolutionaries, and how little they actually knew.

"The Sigil is in Reno, and Doubleshot…is in Oakland," I had said skeptically, looking at the masked figure on Gloric's screen.

"Yes, under," the technomancer said.

"We've been looking for him since the Chinatown incident, eight months at least," I complained.

"Maybe that's part of the problem," he replied. "He's a she."

Vasshka "Doubleshot" Lestrage, the monitor had read. Known only in my circles by her moniker, and wanted in four states for as many auric insurrections. More likely to answer with pistols than with words. And she was in Oakland.

We made our way to the East Bay in the dying light of the afternoon, the western sun backlighting the city behind us and outlining the one hundred and forty-year-old Bay Bridge in auburn fire. There had been no sign of company following us since we left Gloric's neighborhood, but the technomancer set up a private gateway to the network for us just in case.

The gnome's directions took us off the freeway and through a warehouse district abutting the east side of the water. Large, steel-girded buildings stood imposingly around us, glimmering warmly in the sunset. We made our way through them slowly, following Gloric's instructions to an abandoned train station. Alina parked us in an empty lot nearby, engaging the SUV's security systems.

"Couple of things," Gloric said as we walked the short block from the parking lot to the station. His sandals flapped on the asphalt, and he had donned a ridiculously large Giants-themed backpack that bobbed with each step. "One: address Doubleshot only by her nickname. She won't like hearing that you know more about her, or that you learned it from me."

We all nervously murmured our assent.

"And two…" the gnome stopped and looked at me keenly. "Try to look like you belong?"

I looked around at the rest of the party, who nodded knowingly. "What's all this?" I protested.

"You look like a secret agent," Tribe said as Gloric turned and resumed walking.

I glanced down at my outfit, tight-fitting black trousers and shirt under my large overcoat, then at Alina, who snickered not unkindly. I resolved to keep my mouth shut for the encounter.

The gnome led us into the station, a deserted concrete building that was eerie and dark in the dying light. Dusty route maps and departure schedules marked the red- and brown-bricked walls, graffitied almost to the point of being unrecognizable. A broken set of turnstyles bisected the building, leading off to several sets of stairs and elevators that appeared to be out of operation.

Gloric took us through the turnstyles and to a small utility door adjacent to the elevators. The portal was locked by a simple digital code, but the gnome disabled it quickly with a passcode and ushered us into a dank stairwell, securing the door behind us.

"We'll take the back way," he explained, his voice reverberating off of the claustrophobia-inducing walls.

We continued down into the bowels of the station, stopping after two flights of stairs at another, more heavily reinforced gate. The technomancer took a digitab out of his backpack, attempting to unlock the door's safety mechanism. After a few taps, the device beeped morosely.

"This stupid thing," the gnome said irritably, punching the door with a little hand. "Always sticks."

He put away the digitab and produced a tiny ceridium tablet, glowing blue in the near darkness. Pinching it between his fingers, he spoke a series of binary numbers, waving his hand in front of the doorway. The magic left his hands and sought out the locking mechanism, disabling it with a click.

I felt my eyebrows raise in the gloom. Technomancer, indeed.

The gnome pushed open the heavy door with a grunt and led us into a more open space that appeared to be a disused train tunnel. Two passenger platforms sandwiched several sets of electrified rails, looking ancient but surprisingly clear of debris. Light and sounds wafted to us from an entryway recessed into one of the platforms.

"Here we are!" Gloric said cheerily, guiding us to the bar entrance. An arched doorway framed two swinging, wooden half-doors, with an AR sign across them that flashed *Lucky Snake* in my lenses.

We pushed our way into an underground saloon of sorts, in what looked to be a converted maintenance area. A pastiche of tall and short tables littered the room, with low-hanging ceiling lamps that seemed to create more shadows than light. Augmented reality snake-themed graffiti donned the walls to provide some semblance of decoration, and a remodeled jukebox crooned a prehistoric country rock ballad from the corner of the room.

Lucky Snake's clientele looked as hard as its decor. A motley representative of underraces and humans looked up at us as we entered the bar, dark eyes gleaming suspiciously. I felt self-conscious in my standard issue clothing, standing out like a sore thumb in the midst of revolutionaries.

Gloric strode confidently up to the unvarnished bar, signaling the huge auric behind it for a drink. The little gnome could barely see over the counter, but he pulled himself up onto a stool and beckoned us over.

I could feel eyes on me as we walked across the room, and resisted the temptation to use my lenses to look up records for each of the patrons. The place was a treasure trove of rev sympathizers.

"Want anything?" Gloric asked as we joined him at the bar. I shook my head, preferring to keep my wits about me for the time being. Alina ordered a soft drink as Tribe went over to tinker with the jukebox.

I put my back to the bar to survey the room, trying to pick out Doubleshot from the crowd. Most of *Lucky Snake*'s clientele had gone back to their drinking and games of chance, the low rumble of talk and dice filling the concrete room with sound. A table of aurics towards the middle of the room was still giving us the stinkeye. I smiled pleasantly in their direction.

"Where do we find her?" I said to Gloric out of the corner of my mouth, waving cheerily at the revolutionaries.

"Oh, she's here," the gnome said, collecting a handful of shots in his little hands and hopping down off the bar stool. "Just don't want to meet her empty-handed."

Alina and I followed him to the back corner of the room, Buster trailing behind us and sniffing curiously. A table of aurics and humans were in the middle of some Hold 'Em variant, digital chips piled around their cards haphazardly. A dwarf sat on the opposite side, her boots propped up on the table nonchalantly. Her wide brimmed hat shaded her face in the low light, and a cigar glowed red behind her handful of cards.

Her eyes, glistening in shadow, flicked towards me. She spoke one word, the cigar dipping. "Scram."

The rest of the table looked up at us, then back at the dwarf, who tipped her head curtly to the side, revealing a fringe of orange hair beneath her hat. The card players collected their money and left, joining other tables.

"What have we here, Glory?" the dwarf asked, taking a pull at the cigar. Her eyes never left my face.

"Evening, Doubleshot," Gloric said affably, setting the shot glasses on the table and taking a seat. "OK if my friends join us?"

The dwarf clasped the cigar between two meaty fingers, sweeping her hand briskly in accord. The motion opened her jacket front slightly, revealing a thick leather vest and bolo tie, along with an enormous ceridium revolver at her right hip. From reading through her file, I expected there to be an identical one on her left.

Alina and I sat down across from her, Buster plopping down under a chair and falling asleep instantly. I didn't like having my back to the door, but didn't have much choice.

The dwarf put her cigar on its side in an ashtray, blowing out a cloud of smoke and grabbing a couple of shots. Finally taking her eyes off of me, she tossed back the amber liquid.

"What can I do you for?" she drawled in a sooty voice, wiping her mouth with a thick hand.

"Well," Gloric began, skipping pleasantries, "we need someone to take us to the Sigil."

"What for?"

"It's a long story," I spoke, measuring the dwarf with my eyes. She returned my gaze and held it, searching for fear or intimidation. Not finding any, she nodded slowly, taking another two shots.

"Give me the short version," she said.

I looked around me, making sure we were out of earshot from the rest of the room, and sped through the relevant pieces of my story, leaving out any mention of classified information. The dwarf listened patiently, asking a question here and there for clarification.

When I finished, she crossed her arms, sizing me up first, then Alina. Finally, she turned back to Gloric, and a ray of light caught the side of her face, revealing a flush, plump visage and round nose.

"I suppose you're going to tell me I owe you one," she said to the gnome.

The technomancer smiled, toying with one of the shot glasses. "Chinatown didn't fix itself," he said meaningfully. "Besides, it'll be fun!"

The dwarf looked back in my direction, and frowned.

"This bloke giving you trouble, Doubleshot?" I felt a large hand fall on my shoulder.

Out of reflex, I grabbed the hand with my own, standing suddenly and pushing my chair into the offender's kneecaps. I twisted under his elbow, grabbing his wrist with one hand and using it to bend his arm in a Z shape. He grunted in pain, and I continued the motion, flipping him over the chair and onto the floor but keeping my grip on the wrist lock.

As if on cue, the bar's country music skipped, Tribe accomplishing whatever he was trying to do with the jukebox. A dancehall hit, all beats and bass, began to play.

They all attacked at once. The table of aurics and humans had surrounded our little corner, murder in their eyes. I let go of the one on the ground, kicking him in the face as I stepped over him and under the wild swing of the auric on my left, grabbing the back of his shirt and driving my knee into his midsection. He let out a harsh breath as I threw him into the group of attackers, tripping a human woman brandishing an electric club.

A tall half-auric to my right hooked a beer bottle towards my head, and I moved with the motion, punching him in the jaw with my fist as I caught the inside of his wrist with my free hand. I continued my punch over his bicep, folding his arm behind his shoulder and grabbing my own wrist in a two-way lock. Turning my hips, I sent him crashing into a nearby table, using my spin to connect my boot with the chest of another advancing human.

I heard the giveaway hum of ceridium weapons being readied, and came out of my turn to see several of the revolutionaries pulling pistols out of their coats. Most of the bar had cleared away from the immediate vicinity, and Alina was just getting out of her chair and to her feet. The wolf had woken from his nap and was poised to jump into the fray.

My hands leapt to my pistol and nightblade, drawing them smoothly. I trained them on the two closest attackers, but noticed motion in my peripheral vision.

I saw Doubleshot move, and it was unlike anything I had witnessed. She swung a boot off of the table and onto a chair, using it to propel her on top of the table. Impossibly fast, her long-barreled revolvers appeared in her hands, pointing threateningly at the auric on the floor and another next to the table. She couldn't have been more than five feet tall, but she was thick, imposing from her perch on the table.

"Call them off, Largo," the dwarf said quietly.

One of the revolutionaries, a man-sized fellow with greenish skin and a handlebar mustache, squinted at her and spat. "Auric king's looking for this bunch."

"Auric king can wait," Doubleshot replied placidly, with no hint of threat in her voice. Her stance in the dim light gave her the appearance of an executioner, her pistols glowing blue and deadly. "They're under my protection."

The man shifted from one foot to the other, deliberating. There was a tension-filled silence, punctuated ludicrously by Tribe's music emanating from the jukebox. The other bar patrons watched on coolly, and I could see the huge bartender wiping the same glass over and over again, doing his best to ignore us. Tribe unobtrusively made his way through the crowd, smoothly stepping in between tables and chairs.

"Auric king won't like you getting in his way," the man said at last.

"You have five seconds," the dwarf raised her voice slightly, cocking her revolvers.

The auric looked at me, and I recognized him as one of the assassins from *They Might Be Giant*. I must have started, as his eyes twitched.

He let out a breath through his snout, turning back towards Doubleshot and putting away his gun.

"Let's get out of here," he said to the room, taking one last glance at me as he left.

I stashed my weapons as the group cleared out, watching them leave the bar. Alina and Gloric helped put back furniture as Buster looked on, growling softly. Seeing that the danger had passed, Tribe diverted his path and made his way over to the bar.

I turned back to the table, finding Doubleshot back in her seat with her pistols safely stowed and her hat in her hand. Her hair sparkled brilliantly in an orange bun crowned at the top of her head, and her skin was ruddy in the bar light. She had a kind face, with wrinkles at the corner of green eyes and a strong jaw that supported chubby cheeks. Her long auric ears pressed against the side of her head, half a shade lighter than two small horns protruding from her forehead.

The dwarf put her feet up and pulled her hat back on, grabbing her cigar from the ashtray with one hand and a couple of shots with the other. I righted my chair and sat down, reaching for one of the extra glasses.

"Well, um...so!" Gloric said, passing a shot over to me. "What do you think? Can you take us?"

The dwarf looked at me, and I raised my glass in salute. She lifted hers and we drank. It tasted like bourbon, neat and impure, little better than brown moonshine. It burned like fire but I managed to swallow it without coughing.

We slammed the glasses on the table at the same time, and she took a puff from her still-lit cigar.

"If I do this, we're square," she said to Gloric.

The technomancer took a long look at Alina, who inclined her head in assent.

Doubleshot took another moment, crossing her arms again and blowing smoke.

"Alright," she said at length, then looked at me piercingly. "But I want four names wiped from the records when you get access to the database."

"No problem," I croaked, trying to keep the bourbon down. "You have my word."

The dwarf nodded. "I'll take the job."

SIX

The Sigil is a charlatan, a minor player who conflates gambling on information with divination.
  -William D. Karthax, NIGHT Inquisitor General

After some initial skepticism on my part, we ate some of *Lucky Snake*'s surprisingly edible tavern food and returned to collect our truck, which sat alone in the empty parking lot. The evening had deepened into another warm night, a light breeze drifting from the Bay to ruffle my short hair and overcoat.

I felt a pang of jealousy when Doubleshot rode up on her modded hog. Of a classic design, it had all of the bells and whistles of a modern motorcycle with the same deafening sound that had been popular at the turn of the century. It made me miss my cruiser.

"It's a straight shot on the 80 once we get out of Oakland," she explained, pulling up to Alina's driver side window. The dwarf had replaced her large hat for a simple reinforced helmet and kerchief that covered most of her face. "We'll stop in Mystic before crossing the border."

Alina nodded, clarifying with Tribe some ground rules about whose music was allowed to be played while driving, and then followed Vasshka through the harbor district and onto the freeway.

I settled in for the drive, looking to my left towards San Francisco. The city was lit up brilliantly in a multitude of colors across the Bay, which was a deeper shade of black than the sky at this time of night. A crescent of fog had coalesced around the far side of the peninsula, creeping around the northern end to block my view of the Golden Gate. Only the unlit towers of the old bridge peeked through the haze, ominous shadows threatening to pierce the heavens.

As the underrace population began to grow in the thirties and forties, so too did public demand and government funding inflate to support NIGHT involvement at the city, state, and national stages. The U.S. society at large had become used to surveillance at every level, and it was effortless, cathartic even, to turn that scrutiny on what was perceived to be a new set of species.

Pockets of resistance formed to combat the human rights violations that came with the ghettoization and profiling of the growing racial populations in the already impacted urban centers. Some of the demonstrations were peaceful, others less so, but most were uncoordinated on a national scale until Thog'run II, a first-generationer and renowned warrior and revolutionary, claimed his throne in 2063.

The self-professed auric king united the scattered underrace resistance movements under one banner that promised equal rights and protection for all of the new races. Equally important, it provided the physical and philosophical space for an important identity that the disenfranchised underrace communities craved dearly: that of nationhood. It took a few bloody years and a number of uprisings, but Thog'run was able to establish the capital of his empire in the caves beneath the Marin headlands, mockingly close to San Francisco and the seat of NIGHT power in the United States. Just months later, he put out the word that all underraces, from every corner of the Earth, would be welcome and provided for within the new nation of Aurichome.

The auric king called, and the revolutionaries answered. Uprisings cropped up around the world in support of Thog'run's decree, and the underraces flocked to the North Bay, gradually taking over the coast from Sausalito to Fort Bragg. Even humans moved to join the new nation and underground pockets of resistance, buoyed by the sense of freedom afforded by the dictatorship and away from military-controlled democracy. Aurichome provided a release from a world run by armies and corporations, a return to a simpler way of life where all were welcome. The auric king would take anyone, provided that they recognized him as the sole and rightful ruler of Aurichome.

The NIGHTs responded in the way they knew best, but found that even their technologically advanced weaponry and instruments were no match for the aurics' guerilla tactics. Having made a motion to nuke the entire underside of Northern California, their hand was stayed by an uneasy majority in Congress. The government realized it couldn't beat Thog'run in his own territory, so it did the next best thing: made everyone else the enemy.

You wouldn't be able to catch any of the powers that be confessing on holovid, but there was a common understanding that the general underrace populace that remained outside of Aurichome was paying for the perceived sins of Thog'run II. Aurics were stopped at every checkpoint, forced to produce identification upon demand, and denied most basic rights when it came to the law. An auric that had a second cousin living in Aurichome would be called a revolutionary, thrown in the Virtual Penitentiary and most likely forgotten about. The media already had a blueprint for paranoia from the Red and Green Scares of previous decades, and acted accordingly, changing the colors to the blue and white of Thog'run's banner.

The Oxidium epidemic, known colloquially as the rage plague, made matters only worse. The first generation of underraces had been taking the drug experimentally in an attempt to reverse the phenotypic effects of ceridium, which had been shown to work in some clinical trials. It didn't do much outside of giving them a nasty habit and another reason to hate themselves and the way they looked, reinforcing the widely held misconception that they were a different species altogether from *homo sapiens*. When the rage plague began appearing among second-generationers, the underraces suddenly started to need Oxidium to prevent themselves from becoming bloodthirsty monsters, oblivious to everything but their blinding fury. The drug proved to have some usefulness after all, but it was a hollow comfort.

We stopped briefly in Sacramento, a sprawling metropolis that dwarfed San Francisco in space if not population, to grab a few more supplies, and continued east, keeping to the upper traffic whenever possible.

The journey was mercifully uneventful, factories and strip malls zooming past the truck's windows and eventually giving way to the thick evergreen forests of the Sierra foothills. My companions and I kept our own council, lulled into silence by the quiet hum of the SUV's antigravity boosters. Even Buster sat morosely in between the two front seats, chin propped up gloomily on the dashboard.

Alina slowed as she pulled the SUV through Truckee, following Vasshka off the stretch of the freeway that rode through the town. What was once the gateway to the mountain range from the California side was now a government-regulated checkpoint that sat uneasily up against the underrace territory, itself aligned with Aurichome. The dwarf guided us through a series of backroads and back onto the 80 without incident, taking us into the mountains.

The traffic this far east was nonexistent, and after a short time on the freeway, Doubleshot slowed her bike to a crawl, then stopped completely. At her signal, Alina cut the SUV's engine and we all prepared to get out.

"Just a minute, Alina," Gloric said, rummaging through his backpack in the seat next to me.

The gnome produced a small cloth satchel about the size of a grapefruit and embroidered in orange and black.

"In case there's trouble," he offered, handing it to her.

The Pitcher took the bag quizzically, furrowing her delicate brow. Buster and Tribe crowded the front cab as she untied its leather knot, reaching inside to pull out a blue crystal globe about the size of her hand. A molded seam traversed the sphere in a figure eight pattern.

"Is this?" she said slowly.

"In case there's trouble!" the gnome repeated, helping her to press a recessed button on the globe's exterior. At his touch, the mock stitching glowed a brighter blue, revealing a computer chip suspended within the ball like a fly in amber.

"And I?" Alina stammered.

"Throw it like you normally would!" the Technomancer explained, beaming over his invention. "It doesn't have the appropriate coloration, but the weighting is correct. And the best part about it..."

He pressed the button again, and the globe began to hum.

"...Ceridium-veined CPU, with a reinforced microcrystal outer core and spell of returning. It'll be very hard to break, and is programmed to reappear at the point of release on impact."

The Pitcher looked up at Gloric, blue eyes wide.

"Unlimited ammo!" the gnome finished, clapping his hands.

Tribe let out a low whistle into the stunned silence. The wolf sniffed at the globe a couple of times, uninterested.

"Thank you, Glory," Alina said finally, putting a hand on his little shoulder.

"Yes, yes of course," he fussed, blushing a little. "One button to start, two to engage, and another to return to idle."

"Got it," she said confidently, pressing the button again and returning it to the satchel. I was a little jealous.

I gathered my things and we exited the SUV, joining Doubleshot next to her motorcycle. The air was crisp and stars visible above the road, providing a small amount of illumination next to a pale moon.

"Where do we find them?" I asked as we walked up.

"They'll find us," she said, planting her feet firmly and staring towards the east.

We didn't have long to wait. After a few minutes, I could pick out several figures melting out of the shadowed boulders and evergreens at either side of the freeway.

They were rugged, and they were armed. Twenty or more dwarf-sized aurics paced deliberately out into the roadway to encircle us, all manner of axes, picks, rifles, and shotguns brandished openly. They stopped within five paces of us, ceridium weapons glowing at the ready.

As instructed by our guide, we kept our hands empty and visible, which was not easy. Every bone in my body screamed for me to draw my pistol and nightblade and fight my way back to the coast, but I managed to keep myself in check.

"Rodder," Doubleshot acknowledged the dwarf in front of her, a squat fellow with a greying blond beard braided into his bushy hair and curling yellow horns jutting from his forehead.

"Vasshka," he said. "Back already?"

"You know how it is."

"Running to, or from?"

"Neither," our guide said smoothly. "These folks need to speak with the Sigil."

The grizzled dwarf peered at us each in turn, his black eyes unreadable. "Humans?"

"Not really," Doubleshot replied.

Rodder looked us up and down again, then left his post to briskly march over to me.

"What's a fed-loving scab want in dwarf land?" he asked in a low voice, looking up at me. I could smell coriander on his breath.

I held his stare, feeling the eyes of my party and the ring of aurics on me. "Sanctuary," I said.

His bulbous nose twitched as though he was sniffing the truth out of me. "Vasshka?" he barked without turning.

"He's good," Doubleshot said from over his shoulder. "Confused, but good."

Rodder measured me again, then relented, stepping towards our guide. The ring of dwarfs stood placidly, squat sentinels in the road.

"You know the way," he said curtly. Some unspoken message passed between them that I couldn't decipher.

"That I do," Doubleshot agreed. They bowed slightly to each other and Rodder turned on his heel, signaling to his patrol. The dwarves sifted back into the wilderness as quickly as they had arrived.

We got back in the SUV and followed Vasshka through the mountains, seeing the remnants of human civilization as we drove. Here and there, road signs had been cut down or boarded over, and a few abandoned cars littered the shoulder. If there were auric settlements this far west, their entrances were invisible from the freeway. Unlike most of the underrace population, dwarves actually preferred living underground, and made excellent basement renters.

It took a few minutes after crossing the border for us to see the drones. Flitting like fireflies, they zipped across the roadway in the distance, flying unerringly from the left to the right. There were only a few at first, but as we neared the exit to the city center, they grew in number, gliding overhead in a swarm of lights.

The city itself stood like a bright beacon in the inky desert. The abandoned region was dark as far as the eye could see, save the central casino district, which was lit with a kaleidoscope of colors. The drones, almost invisible against the light, were indeed flying in the same direction, but turned in their course when they reached the outer limit of the city.

"They're going in circles," Gloric breathed next to me, pressing his bearded face against the window.

"Have we got a game plan?" Tribe asked as Alina followed Doubleshot off the freeway and into the city center.

"I sure hope so," I said, out of my depth.

We drove in between the towering buildings, skyscraping casinos plastered with AR digads amid brightly lit parking structures and rows of empty restaurants. Fountains spewed forth colorful cascades for no one, and the deserted streets were only more eerie for their brilliance. We drove past a sign that would have once read *Reno - The Biggest Little City in the World*, but its augmented reality wiring now made it display simply, *Reno - The Best City*.

"The marquis," Alina said, pointing as she drove.

I looked outside my window at the moving signs abutting the casinos, each pulsing in my lenses with AR filters. They all creepily read the same message.

"*Welcome, SF Guests*," Tribe read aloud.

"Well, that's nice," Gloric said.

Doubleshot drove into a long, curving driveway adjacent to a large casino, stowing her bike and motioning for us to join her. Alina pulled the SUV in behind the dwarf's bike, parking in what looked like an empty valet zone.

"Brilliant, just brilliant!" Gloric exclaimed, bounding out of the SUV. The rest of us joined him more slowly, taking in the light and color.

The dwarf took us through a set of tinted doors that opened as we approached, blasting us with air conditioning and the deafening clamor of slot machines. The interior of the casino seemed somewhat lively compared to the deserted city, and managed to be even more colorful. Rows upon rows of jackpots, blackjack machines, and other consoles stood protectively around empty card tables and roulette wheels, blaring their jingles noisily. The place smelled of carpets and old tobacco smoke.

"Where is everyone?" Alina wondered out loud.

"Utah, mostly," Vasshka answered, sauntering through the casino. "When we took Nevada, most of them went east, or north to Oregon or Idaho."

"I thought you said the Sigil was in Sparks," I said to Gloric.

The gnome shrugged, looking up at the building's ostentatious chandeliers and ceiling paintings. "He must have liked it here better."

"This way," Doubleshot said, leading us down a side corridor and through an enormous doorway framed in marble that was etched with the word *COLISEVM*.

We walked through two sets of automatic doors into a large, open-air stadium that had been built to resemble an ancient arena. Rows of marble benches encircled a long pitch, which itself was rounded by a dirt running track. Several standing lamps lit the field in radiance, casting the yellowish grass in a warm light.

The arena's inhabitants were a strange motley of electronic visitors. All manner of machines, from ancient personal computers and flashlights to the most modern holodisplays and portable generators littered the field. There were even a few vehicles parked along the track. The drones circled overhead, buzzing.

"God be praised," Gloric declared, picking up his pace. Buster trailed after him, snuffling at the various electronics.

At the center of the pitch sat an old human, dressed simply in a long, flowing robe and wire-framed spectacles. The man was perched cross-legged on an ornate circular pillow, writing furiously at a digital tablet. A long oval of grass surrounded him, free of the electronic clutter save for a small circular device next to him.

The human looked up as we approached, squinting and tugging at his beard. "He said you'd be here ten minutes ago," the man said crabbily.

Vasshka shrugged. "Rodder wanted to talk."

The man threw his hands up irritably, clumsily dropping the digitab. "Dwarves, always meddling," he muttered, fumbling after the tablet.

Alina and Tribe exchanged looks, unsure. Gloric had taken his hat off of his head, mesmerized by the round machine. His heavy backpack looked comical on his small body.

I cleared my throat and stepped forward. "Sigil," I said stiffly, "we need your help to prevent a civil war."

"You've come far, Eskander Aradowsi," a digital voice purred.

I looked down at the circular device. It was a plain, thick grey disc, with a panel of LED lights and buttons and some faded, indecipherable writing. It continued talking, lights flashing as it spoke. "I bid you and your companions welcome, and shall help you if I can."

There are few instances that I can recall being struck completely speechless, having not the slightest idea what to say or how to proceed. This was one of them. Fortunately, Gloric broke the silence with his excitement.

"Oh, Your Grace, it is so very good to meet you!" he said to the machine. "I have been looking forward to this day since my first reprogram!"

"Welcome, Gloric Vunderfel," the little thing buzzed, and the man beside him scribbled at his digitab, recording. "Your reputation precedes you. My drones tell me very good things about your work."

The gnome beamed, and I took a closer look at the device, racking my brain for where I had seen its kind before. Recognition dawned as I remembered seeing a similar contraption in an architecture museum years ago, which had among its collection a number of household appliances that had been used in prior decades. This disc-shaped thing resembled exactly an automatic vacuum device that was purported to be among the first advances towards artificial intelligence. The very premise of true AI had been proved laughable as the science of technology progressed, but it seemed that not everyone knew everything.

Tribe and Alina seemed to catch on about as quickly as I did. I recovered from my surprise, kneeling in front of the machine.

"Your Grace," I said formally, "we have come at great peril to ask for your wisdom on the Inquisitor General's schemes to initiate a war with Aurichome. I intend to expose their plans, but our technomancer," I nodded at Gloric, "has informed us that the information we seek is not accessible through the network."

"Your technomancer knows much, Eskander Aradowsi," the Sigil said, "but he sees facts, not patterns. The Inquisitor General and the auric king do indeed intend war with one another. Yet they are neither what they seem."

I thought about the Sigil's words, holding Buster at arm's length. The wolf was trying to get his snout within sniffing range of the device.

"They're working together?" I asked slowly.

The machine beeped in what must have been a nod. "It will be a tipping point in the battle of races. A watershed moment in the history of nations."

That sparked something. "Project Watershed," I said, looking to the group for support. "What is it?"

"I do not know the answer to this question," the Sigil replied mechanically.

I sat back on my haunches, thinking. Karthax and the auric king being in cahoots would explain the dispensary full of ragers, and the NIGHT-trained auric assassins after us. I couldn't quite grasp what either faction would get out of a full-blown war.

"Tribe Achebe," the Sigil continued. "You too are not what you seem. You must decide which of the paths in front of you to take."

Tribe shifted nervously, reaching into a pocket for his Oxidium, then remembering where he was and dropping his hand. "OK," he said quietly.

The little vacuum turned on its wheels, facing Alina, then Gloric, and Vasshka. It seemed to be calculating.

"Alina Hadzic," it intoned, "fight for that in which you believe, and your aim will always strike true."

The Pitcher breathed in through her nose, considering. She nodded at the Sigil.

It turned to Gloric. "Gloric Vunderfel. My eyes and ears are everywhere, but they have no direction. I would have you be their captain."

The gnome stood like a statue, unmoving. I nudged him gently with my elbow, holding back the wolf with my other hand.

"Yes, yes, Your Grace," Gloric said, falling to a knee. "It would be my honor and privilege."

"Very well," the Sigil droned. "My Scribe will contact you when you return to the coast.

"Vasshka Lestrage," it continued. The dwarf inclined her head soberly.

"You owe me fifty dollars for the Chinatown wager," the Sigil said.

Vasshka smirked, then rummaged in a pocket and handed the Scribe a wad of paper money.

"Amateurs," the old man mumbled as he took the cash, not looking up from his digitab.

"Now," the Sigil said, whirring back towards me. "Do you have the information you need?"

"I think so," I lied. I was having a hard time getting my mind to stop racing, and felt like I had a hundred questions to ask. I picked one.

"If Karthax and the auric king are working together, it would seem that the Inquisitor

General would have everything to gain and nothing to lose, is that correct?"

"Indeed, it would seem that way," the Sigil agreed.

"Unless," Alina chimed in, "Karthax has agreed to give Thog'run something."

"But what would Thog'run want that only Karthax can give him?" I mused aloud.

"The city."

Alina and I turned towards Tribe, taking in his words. Even Gloric looked up from his place of reverence.

The thief shrugged. "What else could he want?"

It made sense. The auric king had land and he had power, but a nation needs a capital. And there would be no better way to address the civilized world as a sovereign than from the seat of anti-underrace leadership itself.

The pieces started to fall into place. Thog'run offers a handful of ragers to the slaughter, Karthax throws a Nightpath into the pot. The media stirs the public into a frenzy, forcing the government's hand into igniting a war with Aurichome. The NIGHTs strategically surrender San Francisco to the auric king, ceding to the lesser evil for the greater good. Thog'run would be given a larger platform, but from Karthax's perspective, it was one that could be controlled and contained. The plan would doubly allow the NIGHTs to save face by not appearing to have diplomatic relations with the revolutionaries.

A plan began forming in my head, but I would need to gain access to the secured data drive, and that would require going into the lion's den. I knew who would be protecting it.

"Agrid the Destroyer," I said to the Sigil. "What role does he play in all of this?"

The vacuum buzzed, calculating. It turned to the left, then to the right, and back again. The stadium hummed with the sound of different appliances.

"You may ask him yourself," the Sigil said, pointing itself towards the marble entryway. "He is here."

SEVEN

The most experienced mancers believe ceridium to be the axis upon which all magic turns. The uninitiated see it as a mystical element that is foreign to nature. Neither of these opinions is accurate.

-The Sigil of Sparks

I wheeled back towards the arena's entrance, just in time to see the assassin stalk through the marble doorway, lackeys in tow. He walked with single-minded purpose, snaking in between the sundry machines with his crimson eyes unerringly upon us. His white skin appeared ghostly pale in the stadium light, and I counted twenty-two underrace henchmen behind him.

I drew my nightblade and pistol as they approached, and without a word of communication, my companions followed suit. Tribe pulled out a semi-automatic ceridium rifle from somewhere, and Alina palmed the blue sphere, initializing its processor and return function. Gloric pushed a button on his digitab, and four robotic arms slithered out of his huge backpack, reaching over his little shoulders to train what looked like small missiles on the advancing assassins. Buster, almost as large as the little gnome, lowered himself to the ground in a ready position, growling. Only Vasshka remained still, crossing her arms lazily in front of her.

"Welcome, Agrid Ogreson," the Sigil said as the Destroyer reached at the edge of the oval. The auric stood waiting, staring at me.

"I have no quarrel with you, Sigil," the assassin said. His voice was smooth but menacing, like a poisonous gas slipping free from a canister.

"Nor I with you or your masters," the vacuum replied, its lights turning a shade of red that matched the entromancer's overcoat.

"Then turn these ones over to me."

"I cannot do that."

The entromancer took a step into the oval, reaching into his crimson overcoat for something.

The Sigil's response was immediate. Dozens of mechanical and ceridium artillery weapons rose out of the thousands of machines in the arena, pointing at the assassins. They buzzed and clicked, filling the coliseum with power.

"I will not have bloodshed in my sanctuary," the Sigil intoned.

The Destroyer stopped in his tracks. I could hear the Scribe behind me pause in his writing.

Slowly, the assassin removed his hand from his coat, holding it up in a signal of acquiescence. His red eyes burned holes into mine.

"Very well," he said. "We shall wait outside."

The auric turned on his heel confidently, signaling to his party. The assassins left as quickly as they had come, disappearing into the casino.

I started breathing again, putting away my weapons. The others did the same, and the Sigil's weapons lowered themselves among the arena's appliances.

"Rude," said the Scribe, resuming his scribbling.

"I apologize for the intrusion," the Sigil spoke. "Yet I cannot protect you outside of these walls."

I nodded, understanding. "You have already helped us immensely, Your Grace. I appreciate your help."

"And I appreciate your honesty, Eskander Aradowsi. May you see the daylight again. My Scribe will be in contact with you, if that is the case."

We said our goodbyes to the Sigil, Gloric genuflecting again. As we walked towards the entryway, Tribe hurried to jump out in front of the group.

"Wait, we're just going to go out there and fight them?"

"That's the plan," I said.

"No tactics? Strategy? Nothing?" he complained, his long ears standing on end.

I shrugged. "I usually work alone."

"I have an idea," Alina spoke up. It had been a long time since I had worked with a group, but the half-auric had done two tours in the military.

She explained her plan quickly, coming up with ideas as she spoke. We made adjustments as questions came up, but formed a working strategy within a few minutes.

We left the arena and I took Tribe, Vasshka, and Buster as Alina and Gloric headed in a different direction. My group walked back towards the casino area, still jangling with sound.

They were waiting for us in the central foyer, a large circle that led off into four directions. Slot machines and card tables encroached on either side of the four paths, with each row blocked off by one of the assassins. The Destroyer stood patiently in the middle of the foyer, two of his lackeys standing behind him with their weapons drawn.

"How did you find us?" I asked as we entered the circle.

The auric lifted the side of his mouth in what I presumed to be a snicker. "Just followed the trail."

I hid my confusion as best as I could. Gloric had removed the tracers from our digitabs and put us on a hidden network, and we had been careful to move covertly. It was unlikely that anyone heard our conversation in *Lucky Snake*, but our little altercation could have notified any number of underground networks of our presence. For someone with the right instruments, it would have been a simple matter to track us from there.

I decided to leave the issue alone for now, but needed to buy time. "So this is it, then? Betray your own people for a handful of government cash?"

The auric snorted, his enforcers moving around nervously. He didn't seem to be the laughing type.

"Do not speak to me of traitors," he said, motioning vaguely towards me. I had to stop myself from reaching for my weapons.

"Why?" I pressed. "Too close to home? Or is Karthax paying you well enough to not care?"

The Destroyer didn't rise to the bait. He coughed, or chuckled. It was difficult to tell the difference.

"You are too myopic to see past your own version of the truth," he said, closing his hand into a fist. "The world is changing, and one has to change with it to survive."

"So you would be a traitor to your own race to survive?"

"*Do not speak to me of traitors!*" he yelled, taking a step forward. His hands flexed dangerously, power building at his fingertips. The other assassins looked at each other apprehensively. To my eternal gratitude, my companions held their ground. I was hitting a nerve.

"What, then?" I asked, trying to keep him talking but without getting myself killed. "Why are you doing this?"

The auric let out a breath, visibly gathering himself. "Do not speak to me of traitors," he said again, more calmly. "I've read your file. You don't have much moral high ground."

I lifted my palms appeasingly, unperturbed. "I've got nothing to hide."

"That's your problem, you don't see your own hand in the destruction of our people."

I furrowed my brow, genuinely confused.

"First agent of underrace blood to join the NIGHTs?" he said pointedly. I shook my head, not understanding. He wasn't wrong; I was a quarter auric from my father's side of the family, but it wasn't any secret. My angular facial features and pointed ears made certain that anyone who met me knew my racial background, which got me into some places, and out of others.

The assassin snorted again. "You're the true government's pet. An auric who's so self-hating that he doesn't mind locking up his own people to preserve the status quo."

I shrugged uncomfortably. I had been called worse, and on the same topic. For whatever reason, the assassin's comment sat uneasily with me, in light of everything I had learned from Gloric and the Sigil.

"Just trying to survive," I said, echoing his earlier comment.

He smirked, and despite our situation on opposite sides, I felt a sense of understanding, or something akin to respect, transfer between us.

It passed quickly. The auric's expression changed, eyeing our little group.

"Have your friends reconsidered their allegiances?" he said, noting the absence of Alina and Gloric.

"They've chosen sanctuary," I said, noting a buzz in my earpiece signaling that the others were in position.

"They will rot in that arena. I have men and women posted at every exit of this casino."

He looked to the side, speaking to his hit squad. "Keep the Nightpath and thief; kill the others."

"That won't be necessary," I said, drawing his attention back towards me.

A streak of blue flashed from his left, blindingly fast. The entromancer had just enough time to speak a word of power and raise his hand, creating a small transparent shield that deflected the bolt into one of his underlings. The Pitcher's sphere struck the lackey in the chest, sending him crashing into a craps table before disappearing back into Alina's hand.

Half of the assassins turned to face the new threat, while the other half readied to open fire on my group. From the opposite direction, I could hear a code being pronounced, all ones and zeroes, followed by a flash of blue. One third of the enforcers' weapons clanked loudly, jammed and useless by Gloric's technomancy.

The gnome appeared hovering over a row of slot machines, the bottom of his sandals glowing with some kind of ceridium-powered propellant. Another cobalt curveball streaked through the air to take out a short auric holding two machine guns, and the rest of us burst into action.

As we had rehearsed, Tribe and the wolf dashed in opposite directions in between the adjacent tables of chance, leaving Vasshka and I to deal with the Destroyer and his cronies. The ones with weapons still working opened fire, but not before we rolled out of the way behind a couple of slot machines. Bullets pelted the machines, ringing incongruously against the blaring casino sounds. I nodded at the dwarf as I drew my nightblade and a ceridium capsule.

Doubleshot nodded back, springing from her crouch and back into the foyer. In one smooth motion, she drew both of her long pistols, firing them twice as her leap took her horizontal. Two assassins fell as she turned her jump in to a roll, spinning and firing twice again. Two more assassins hit the ground as she rolled a second time, through another row of machines and out of sight.

I used the distraction to run around the slot machine, chanting and tossing the capsule in front of me. A shimmering black portal appeared in front of me, wisps of shadow trailing from its corners. I jumped through it as bullets fired upon my position, orienting myself towards the Destroyer, who was moving his hands through a spell.

I came through the shadowgate a few feet behind him, my nightblade raised for a killing blow. Unthinkably fast, the auric turned and completed the casting, his red coat whipping behind him. I ducked to avoid a spray of animal teeth and wrapped candies, which turned into some kind of metal spikes as they flew through the air above me.

I turned as I dropped, sticking a leg out and catching the backs of his knees, tripping him. He used his fall to tumble backwards, jumping nimbly to his feet. I saw movement from the corner of my eye and threw myself to the side and behind a booth emblazoned with augmented reality dollar signs and images of digital poker chips. Ceridium bullets plunked into the metal as a pair of aurics fired at me, but Gloric zoomed into view and fired a couple of rockets from his shoulders, taking them both out and a good chunk of the carpeted floor with them.

From my vantage, I could see Alina far down one of the aisles leading off of the foyer, sending pitch after pitch at the assassins advancing upon her, her wild hair tucked under her cap and eyes focused straight ahead. A pair of gnomes creeped through the machines around her, visible only as they passed in between the gaps in rows. I wanted to call out to alert her to the danger, but then saw Tribe's stalking form headed in their direction, and a tuft of fur moving to intersect. The gnomes' screams a few moments later assured me of Alina's safety.

I turned back to the foyer to see Doubleshot backing out of another lane, firing her pistols two at a time at the Destroyer. The assassin had equipped what looked to be a retractable ebony spear, blue ceridium currents swirling up and down its length. He deflected Vasshka's shots one by one with the staff and a wave of his hand, somehow still casting.

More henchmen came bounding into the foyer from the casino's exits, having been alerted of the melee. Doubleshot was forced to shift her attention off of the entromancer, picking off aurics with cobalt blasts from her pistols.

The Destroyer finished his spell, making a wild call that sounded like a crow cawing, dropping an egg to the ground and crushing it with his foot. His skin shivered, shifting weirdly and hardening into an interlaced network of silvery hexagons.

The conjuring was timed to perfection, settling in place just as a zipping Gloric flew past the assassin, rockets firing. They exploded against the entromancer's armor, destroying chunks of it but leaving his body underneath it mostly unscathed. Tracking Gloric's receding form, the Destroyer sent the black and blue spear sailing through the air, harpooning the technomancer like an eel. The gnome shrieked, veering off course and crashing into a table.

"Glory!" Vasshka screamed plaintively, planting a couple of bullets into a troll as she ran in the gnome's direction.

I drew my pistol and moved around the kiosk, firing at the entromancer to get his attention. It worked a little too well. One of the ceridium bullets blasted against his head, destroying the armor and revealing his face, and the other grazed an exposed portion of his arm. He staggered with the blows but called upon his spear, which returned to him in an instant.

A shadow appeared behind him, and my heart fell into my gut.

"Tribe, don't!" I called uselessly.

The assassin turned as Tribe sprung from his hiding place, dagger exposed and ready to strike. The Destroyer caught him by the throat with one hand, squeezing and tossing him across the foyer. The thief landed with a groan and a sickening crunch at the feet of two hulking enforcers.

"Take him!" the entromancer yelled at them, turning back towards me.

Our eyes met, and I sheathed my pistol, knowing it to be useless. I gripped my nightblade in two hands, advancing towards him slowly.

He didn't give me the opportunity. The auric took two steps and then lunged, driving his spear down towards me like a pioneer striking a flag into the heart of the earth. I parried it desperately with my sword, letting him move in closer. I struck out with my elbow, hitting his exposed face with a satisfying crack.

He took the blow, changing his grip on the ceridium-laced spear to clock me under the chin with the butt end. My head exploded in pain but I danced backwards, grabbing the weapon and pulling him off balance. I spun in place, turning my hips to swing the nightblade under his guard. He moved, but not quickly enough, and I tore a slice through his coat and under his outstretched arms. He accepted the wound with a grunt, and fired off a string of commands in an unintelligible language.

Two heavy wooden logs materialized in the air before me, swinging in my direction. I managed to parry one of them with my sword, but the other caught me in the solar plexus, driving the wind out of me and sending me to the floor. The back of my head hit the ground with the impact, and I could feel the nightblade clatter out of my hands.

My vision blurred, and time slowed to a crawl. As if in slow motion, I could see Tribe to my right struggling against his captors, calling my name. Across from me, I saw Vasshka standing over Gloric's lifeless form, roaring in anger and firing at the attackers two at a time. Above me, the entromancer hovered, the ebony and sapphire spear raised threateningly.

Some conscious part of me took a small amount of pride in seeing his bloody face and chest, knowing that he could indeed be hurt. Behind him, I could see Buster racing towards us, but I knew he would be too late.

The entromancer spat a tooth on the ground, then drove his spear at me. I saw a streak of blue, and then nothing.

EIGHT

It is a drug. It is not an antidote; it is not a medication. It is not a solution to our condition, for we have no condition that needs solving. It is a narcotic, nothing more.

-Thog'run II, King of Aurichome

The blackness was a soothing comfort that wrapped around me like a thick blanket. I was at the bottom of a well, a pit deep within the earth, a time capsule in the deepest reaches of space. My world stood unmoving, blessedly quiet, incomparably dark.

Every once in a while, a painful light would shine in the darkness, setting the world to spinning and making me aware of my existence, a floating nothingness in the vacuum. I collected the shadows around me, trying to settle back in the tranquility.

The darkness would no longer respond to my touch. The light became more insistent, a throbbing ache that replaced my comforting blanket and rocketed me through space, ever upwards. I shot out of my unconscious state like a bat out of hell, gasping for air like a drowner unwillingly being pulled out of water.

Everything hurt. My head swam, my ribs were on fire, and the rest of my body felt like it had been devoured by a dragon and spit back up. I tried to blink the bleariness out of my eyes, to no effect, and settled for looking through a blurry white haze for a few minutes.

I relied on my other senses to ascertain my surroundings. The air was warm on my skin, with a light breeze, and smelled of mulch and metal. I could feel grass and dirt beneath me, and hear a slight ringing and whirring in the background. By the foul taste on my tongue, it seemed as if something had crawled in my mouth and died there.

I was outside, the sun mercilessly bathing my surroundings in brightness and sending needles through my sensitive vision. I tried to push myself up on my elbows, but my head whirled again. I turned to the side and retched, hoping that I wasn't lying on someone's fine outdoor furniture.

I rolled over to lay on my back, content to just breathe and let the sun warm me. Slowly, I began to regain consciousness, first remembering who I was, then recalling the fight that had knocked me out. Everything else was a blank.

With a herculean effort, I ventured another try at sitting up. My head ached and my chest burned, but I was able to push myself into a half-lying, half-sitting position and stay there. I blinked some more, allowing the world to come into focus.

I was back in the Sigil's sanctuary, shirtless and surrounded in a sort of room formed by automated washer-dryers. Drones flitted in a halo overhead, intermittently blocking the sun. Across from me sat Gloric, his shirt torn and an ugly bruise staining his portly dark midsection. The rounded cross at his throat looked heavy against his chest.

"Good morning," he said as I moved. "Or should I say, good afternoon."

I grunted, my tongue thick. I rubbed my eyes with my fingers and rolled inelegantly into a full sit, leaning against a washing machine.

"You look terrible," the gnome added, coughing weakly.

"You're one to talk," I retorted, feeling gently at the back of my head. It had been bandaged, but was still tender. "Alina fix you up?"

"Yes, praise God. She's resting; it took a lot out of her."

"I'm not surprised." I wasn't. Gloric's was a mortal wound, and it would have exhausted Alina's deepest reserves of energy - and most likely, her ceridium - to heal it.

"She's hardly left your side, until about a half an hour ago."

I grunted again, checking my ribs. They were bandaged as well, my shirt and long coat carefully folded on the ground where my head had been resting. My chest hurt immensely, but my ribs felt bruised and not broken.

I let out a sigh, resting. Some unknown amount of time passed, and I must have slept, for when I woke up, the sun had moved and Doubleshot had joined Gloric across from me. They chatted in low tones, the dwarf sitting amicably with her booted feet crossed in front of her. She had donned her hat again, pulling down her kerchief so that she could lazily smoke a cigar.

"Well, look who decided to wake up," she teased as she saw me move. Gloric chuckled, then coughed.

"What time is it?" I asked irritably, not having the strength to look for my digitab or initialize my lenses.

"Quarter five," the dwarf drawled.

An elusive memory nagged at me. I opened one eye to look at Vasshka. "Same day?"

She nodded.

I let out another sigh of relief. I had been out for less than twenty-four hours, which was important because of some reason that I couldn't remember. We had to go somewhere to do something, and time was of the essence.

None of it seemed as important as a hot meal and a shower at the moment.

As if in response to my train of thought, my stomach growled loudly. I clutched at it, starving.

"Hungry?" Gloric asked.

I nodded. "Like never before."

Vasshka helped Gloric slowly get to his feet, and they left the little area, still chatting. I made a weak effort at rummaging through my clothes for the Oxadrenalthaline, but couldn't find it. A short time later, Buster padded carefully into the makeshift room, walking up to me to lick my face. I dug a hand into his coat, scratching him.

The sight and feel of him jolted my memory, and I remembered everything. The wolf running, too late, to my rescue as the entromancer stood above me, ready to deliver the killing blow. Vasshka fending off attackers while protecting a prone Gloric. Tribe being dragged from the casino, pleadingly calling my name in anguish. Alina's sphere smashing into the side of the assassin's face, spoiling his strike.

Tribe. We had to get to Tribe before they did any more damage.

I used the wolf's strong frame to support me as I pushed myself to my feet. Gingerly, I gathered my belongings and slipped back into my shirt and overcoat. It hurt, but felt good to move.

I wandered from the little infirmary towards the center of the arena, smelling food. The others had ransacked the casino's non-perishable supplies, preparing a substantial meal of canned goods and flash-frozen food. The Scribe stood behind a portable induction stove, stirring a pot with one hand while using his finger to scribble on his digitab. The rest of the group sat in the grass oval, eating.

Alina looked up as we approached, Buster running over to put his face in a bowl of scraps. The Pitcher handed me a plate filled with food, and made room next to her for me to sit down.

"Thanks," I said gratefully, gently lowering myself to the floor. I put my hand on her arm as she passed me the food.

"And thanks," I added. She caught my eye and my meaning, smiling slightly.

"Don't mention it."

I set to inhale my food, taking large bites and washing it down with a cup of water. It was tepid, but felt soothing on my parched throat.

I noticed something missing. "Where's the Sigil?" I asked around a mouthful of beans.

The Scribe piped up, not looking way from his stirring or digitab. "Even His Grace tires of company," he said meaningfully.

We finished our meals in silence, and a bit more quickly, thinking that we had already overstayed our welcome. I stretched a little, feeling strength slowly returning to my body.

"So," I said at last, "what happened after I went out?"

"*She* happened," Alina said, pointing at Doubleshot with a piece of bread. "Demon with legs, that one."

If Vasshka was impressed or embarrassed by the compliment, she didn't show it. "They kept coming, but we held them off. We pulled you guys into the sanctuary and Alina looked after your wounds."

"The assassin?" I asked, knowing the answer.

"Had half of his face almost cave in, courtesy of our Pitcher here," Gloric said proudly, his tiny hands resting comfortably on his belly. "Cast a spell and disappeared. The rest of the rabble routed after him."

"Wait, how do you know?" I objected, confused. "Weren't you dead?"

"I have cameras throughout this city, and others, Eskander Aradowsi," the Sigil buzzed, rolling into view from a nearby pathway between the machines. "My captain now has access to most of them."

I stuck out a lip, impressed. Setting down my plate, I cleared my throat, asking the question on everyone's mind.

"What about Tribe?"

Only Doubleshot would meet my gaze. "They got him," she said.

I had suspected as much, but my heart sank nonetheless. I knew what they would do, and it would break him.

"We have to move," I declared, starting to get up. "If we leave now, we can be back in the city by nightfall-"

"To do what?" Alina interrupted me, looking up at me defiantly.

"Get back to the NIGHT headquarters," I sputtered defensively. "They'll have taken Tribe to the VPen, so we can grab him and then the data drive-"

"And how do you propose we do that?" she said, rising to her feet. "You're injured, we're all exhausted, and Glory's out of commission."

"Well, I-" the gnome began to protest.

"Even if we were at our full strength," Alina raged, "I don't see how we'd manage to break into a fortified island of government superagents, fight our way to the VPen, locate the data drive, and escape with our lives."

"I have a friend on the inside," I said, "she could help us to-"

"You don't get it, Nightpath! Some of us gave up fighting because we stopped believing in what we were fighting for. You've dragged us into your mess, and want us to help you clean it up."

I opened my mouth to respond, and shut it. I didn't have much to say to that. I looked to the others for support, but didn't receive any.

"Listen," I said placatingly, "I realize that I've made a lot of assumptions, starting with coming to you for help. And I understand that because of your involvement with me, you're now all targets - with the exception of Doubleshot, who was already a wanted fugitive."

Vasshka tipped her hat in acknowledgement.

"But there's only one way out of this, and it's through the top," I continued. "If we want to save Tribe from certain torture, clear our names, and avoid a war, we have to get into Alcatraz."

"The world doesn't need a savior, Nightpath," Alina said quietly, relenting a little.

"I'm not looking to be one."

"Can I say something here?" Gloric chimed in. Seeing no protests, he continued. "Getting into the NIGHT base won't be *that* much trouble. I can access most of the security protocols fairly easily, if the Nightpath's associate can do the rest. We'd only need a distraction to draw the NIGHTs' attention from our entry."

"That may not be necessary, Gloric Vunderfel," the Sigil said. "Your team's actions have spurred the Inquisitor General and auric king to action, earlier than planned. Their machinations are already coming to fruition."

That gave us pause. If Karthax and Thog'run had set their plans into motion, the city could be under siege, even overrun, within a matter of days. The NIGHTs were formidable, and could enlist the aid of the military and local enforcement if necessary, but the Inquisitor General hadn't gotten to his position of power without making certain connections along the way. If he wanted the city to be turned over to the underraces under the pretense of battle, it would happen.

"How long do we have?" I asked the Sigil.

"My eyes show revolutionary movement underground, and increased NIGHT activity," the vacuum beeped. "Estimated time before impact is three hours."

I quickly initiated my lens display and pulled out my digitab to sync it with the network, trusting in Gloric's protective subnetwork and knowing the assassin knew where to find me, in any case. Several messages from Madge and Striker popped up, along with quite a few other alerts. I ignored them and pulled up a display, looking at the news.

A number of articles appeared, detailing the dispensary bombing, the loss of a NIGHT operative to revolutionaries who sacrificed their own in the blast, and the brief ensuing military preparations. Karthax was depicted making an onscreen speech to Congress, alongside a picture of me in uniform and another of the auric king looking menacing. They had made a martyr out of me, and had been well-primed for war after decades of human-underrace tension. My reported death was the camel's straw.

I put away the digitab and addressed the group. "We have to stop it," I said, putting confidence in my voice. "Not because we're the best equipped, and not because it's our responsibility."

I paused, letting them digest my words. "But because no one else will.

"I may have gotten you all into this," I continued, "but it's bigger than me, and I need your help to fix it. I can get to Tribe and the data drive, but I'll need you to cover me. If not for me, do it for your friend. And if not him, do it for the city."

I looked around at my companions, trying to make eye contact with each of them. "Will you help me?"

Doubleshot was the first to respond, chuckling. "You had me at 'leave now.'"

I grinned, then looked at Gloric. The gnome cocked his head to the side. "I wouldn't be much of a captain if I didn't!" he said. I liked his attitude. "I may not be much help at the moment, but I'm in."

I turned towards the Pitcher, knowing that I needed her, more than the rest. "Alina?"

Her face was placid, but I could see emotions warring behind her blue eyes. Her freckles were pretty in the sunlight.

"OK," she said at last, giving in. I flashed her a smile, which she returned with a little reluctance.

I looked from Buster, who had fallen asleep, to the Sigil. "Thank you, Your Grace, for your help and protection."

"You are welcome, Eskander Aradowsi," the machine said. "Fare well, and expect communication from my Scribe."

We said our goodbyes, making our way back through the arena and casino to our parked vehicles, which had thankfully been left alone by the assassins. Vasshka and Alina plotted a course back to San Francisco, and we headed through the mountains towards the setting sun.

Our little caravan slowed as we reached Mystic, Doubleshot noticing something in the roadway. My stomach turned as I saw what it was. The dwarven patrol lay in heaps across the freeway along with three times their number in the entromancer's assassins. Alina and Vasshka set about the gruesome task of searching for life, finding none. It was no stretch of the imagination to determine who was responsible.

We helped Vasshka build a cairn with the nearby rocks, burying the dwarves beneath with their weapons. She stood stolidly for a few minutes as we prepared to leave.

"I'm sorry," I said as I walked up behind her.

"He was my brother," she said stoically. I assumed she meant Rodder.

"I'm...really sorry," I repeated dumbly, tentatively putting my hand on her shoulder. She accepted it gratefully, reaching out to gently touch the cairn.

We gathered ourselves and drove away, leaving the assassins in the road behind us.

The drive was quiet, more so without Tribe's music or chattering. When we had made our way around Truckee, we began assembling our plan for assaulting the NIGHT headquarters, speaking to Vasshka through the SUV's audio system and trying to put the gruesome sight of the dwarves out of our minds.

By all accounts, San Francisco would be a warzone by the time we returned. The auric king's army would have made their way under the city, drawing on its revolutionary safe houses to capture strategic and vulnerable locations. The Coast Guard and SFPD would put up a fight, and the NIGHTs would be called in almost immediately, but Karthax would have already prepared a tactical retreat, falling back to headquarters. There would be a brief window of time when most of the operatives would be in the field, and I had no idea what they planned to do with Alcatraz when Thog'run had his run of the city.

It seemed hard to believe that the Inquisitor General, a man who had worked all his life in the service of humans, would be willing to give even an inch to the opposing side, even if that served a greater purpose. I suppose you just don't know people.

My own emotions were a whirl. Like most halfies, fourthies, eighthies, and so on, I wasn't used to self-identifying as either human or auric, having spent so much time in the company of both, and rarely being accepted by either. The pluralist allure of Aurichome had never held much sway for me, as it appeared from the outside to be too absolute of a dictatorship for my liking. Yet, I was slowly become acquainted with the appeal of picking a side and sticking with it, if only to put to rest the constant, if not always perceptible, feeling of alienation. I couldn't deny the simple sense of belonging that being a NIGHT had afforded me, but it was no real community. I wasn't sure what I would do or where I would go if we were indeed able to secure the data drive and clear my name, but I hadn't been able to think past that point just yet.

The plan, if it could be called that, would be to utilize the revolutionary assault as a distraction to gain access to the NIGHT headquarters. For the short period of time before the retreat, Alcatraz would be operated by a skeleton crew, allowing us to gain access to the perimeter fairly easily, with the help of Gloric's technomancy. Vasshka and the gnome would provide cover support for me and the Pitcher, giving the two of us time to break into the facility, if Gloric's keycodes worked properly. We'd still need Madge's help for some of the security systems, but I was sure she'd come to our aid. We had been through almost everything together, and I trusted her with my life.

Having gained entrance to Alcatraz, Alina and I would head to the VPen and then the mainframe, which was my best guess for where the secured data drive was stored. I hoped that hitting the VPen first would allow us to free other prisoners of war and create a secondary distraction. I had no idea what we would do if the data drive wasn't where I thought it was, but put that thought out of my mind. It had to be there, and we would use it to prove our innocence, along with the falsehood of Karthax's war.

I chuckled ruefully at the irony of breaking into the island fortress, which had years before been a federal penitentiary, and still housed a number of VPens. Most people had spent their time trying to get *out* of the place.

I didn't want to put Alina in the line of fire, but she was the only one that could heal Tribe's wounds, or anyone else in the VPen. Vasshka and Gloric would have to fend for themselves, but I had every confidence in the dwarf's ability to keep them both safe.

I shuddered to think of what they were putting Tribe through. Originally created as a band-aid solution for the limited space in local jails and federal prisons, the government had leveraged entertainment-based virtual reality technology to create VPens. Tiny chips that, with the appropriate audiovisual hardware and security systems to keep the subject in place, could create a virtual penitentiary anywhere, programmed with the requisite punishment. Lawbreakers could be locked up in smaller spaces, with minimal supervision, forced to re-experience whatever virtual judgment was decreed necessary.

Punishments were regulated by the judicial system, but in the wrong hands, the chip could be used to do a lot worse. The VPen was intended to give a shoplifter the repeated virtual experience of being apprehended while in the act of stealing, with the stomach-churning feeling of being thrown behind bars, again and again. It was supremely effective, allowing judges to give lighter sentences and penitentiaries to house more people for a shorter amount of time. Over time, however, applications began to be developed that would go beyond the original scope of implementation, particularly under the auspices of internal defense.

The NIGHTs would describe it as interrogative questioning; the revolutionaries called it torture. The public, tired after generations of such discussions, didn't care.

With an unrestricted VPen, they could get Tribe to say anything they wanted him to. They would put a visor and headphones on him and let him sit in his own filth while they played scenario after virtual scenario through his chip. They would burn him, they would break him, they would humiliate him. And when they were done, he would swear on his life that he was a revolutionary, if his captors chose it.

I hoped against hope that we would get to him before that happened. We had to.

We made it back to the Bay Area around midnight, our stop in Mystic having pushed back our intended travel time. By the time the Bay Bridge came into view, we already had some idea of what we were up against.

At first glance, it appeared as though the city was on fire. Orange flames could be spotted, engulfing several of the smaller downtown buildings visible from our vantage. Upon closer examination, it looked like there were as yet only minor pockets of fighting that had broken out, which were corroborated by reports that Gloric was receiving on his digitab. Red and blue lights flashed on the bridge, local police and NIGHT vehicles blocking the roadway. Alcatraz stood solemnly in the middle of the inky Bay to our right, its ivory towers bathed in emergency red lights.

"Bridge is blocked," I stated the obvious.

"Which way do you want me to go?" Doubleshot's voice came through the truck's speakers.

"There's a harbor in the city of Berkeley, on this side of the Bay," I said, thinking out loud. "We can commandeer some water cruisers from the docks, but there will be security."

"On it," Gloric said from the back seat, tugging his massive backpack out from underneath Buster. He pulled out a portable keyboard and strapped it around his body, beginning to type.

Alina swung off of the 80 towards Berkeley, following Vasshka onto a frontage road towards the marina. I made a quick call to Madge, needing her help with what we were about to do.

Her voice reverberated in my ear almost immediately.

"Eskander?" she sounded worried.

"Madge, can't talk, being tracked. Need you to let me into HQ when I give you the signal."

"Eskander, I-"

"No time!" I barked. "Wait for my signal."

I hung up, hoping that Gloric's security measures held, and that our brief call wasn't long enough to be traced.

I hesitated, unsure of what I was about to do, but put my trust in my instincts and sent off another message.

We made it to the harbor in no time, several NIGHT cruisers and police cars racing past us in the opposite direction. I turned in my seat to give Gloric a look.

"That you?" I asked.

The gnome nodded happily. "They seem to think there's been an incursion on our side of the Bay."

I snickered, glad he was on our side.

The harbor was mostly deserted, with only a few parked cars and very few personnel at this time of night. Tall oak trees swayed in a fresh night breeze, silent sentinels in the otherwise quiet marina. We stashed the SUV and Vasshka's motorcycle a few blocks away from the docks, walking the rest of the way.

I had thought that we would need to move a little slowly for Gloric's sake, but the little auric proved to be made of sturdier stock, and kept pace with the rest of us. I injected myself with some Oxadrenalthaline to mask my own injuries for a few hours. Hopefully we wouldn't need more than that.

There were only a handful of police officers and two NIGHT heavy cruisers still stationed at the docks. The two factions sat as far away from each other as possible in the large parking lot in front of the shipyard, visibly wanting nothing to do with one another. I employed a shadowspell to send the police officers chasing a fleeing silhouette, and Gloric used his keyboard to override one of the cruisers' remote driving systems. The gnome guided the vehicle away from the harbor and into the city proper, leaving the other cruiser to drive after it in pursuit.

I was starting to think that this was going to be easy, and did not like that feeling.

The docks were divided into several different sections, from a larger, metal-wrought wharf that housed large transportation ships to more moderate, wooden piers where privately owned yachts and houseboats bobbed. We easily located a vacant water cruiser, using Gloric's skills to disable the digital security and power it up. It was a medium-sized vehicle, modeled like a speedboat crossed with a waverunner, with a ceridium engine that could do a hundred knots in open water.

I took the captain's seat, preferring that the technomancer focus his efforts on deflecting any resistance we might meet on the water. It was only five or six miles to the island, and most of the NIGHTs' attention would be turned towards the battle in San Francisco, but I wasn't willing to take any chances. Based on the state of the city and our current location, I estimated we had about an hour to get into the base, grab Tribe and the data drive, and get out of there.

I looked around at my teammates, then back at the glimmering city and the white towers of

Alcatraz. The Bay Bridge loomed bright to our left, and I could hear the faint sound of sirens on the wind. A light spray from the black water beneath began to hit us as I maneuvered out of the harbor and into the Bay. Straight ahead, behind the NIGHT headquarters, the Golden Gate Bridge stood dark and vacant, brooding solemnly in the empty night, a silent reminder of what was at stake.

One hour to save the city, perhaps the world. It would have to be enough.

NINE

*If I am a charlatan, I have fooled even myself,
believing that despite my form and origination, I
yet possess the capacity for thought, emotion,
and morality.*

-The Sigil of Sparks

One mile out from Alcatraz, we almost drowned. We had come to the outer perimeter of NIGHT security, just outside the visible range of a solitary cruiser. We were lucky that the whole of the facility's attention was focused in the opposite direction towards the city, but still had to move carefully.

I turned our vehicle broadside to the island, having made sure all of the visible lights were off and reminding myself to thank the Sigil that what few drones were left were being used elsewhere. Knowing how the battle would play out, Karthax would move all of his forces into the city, unconcerned that the auric king would venture as far east as the NIGHT headquarters.

"Here's good," Gloric said, rummaging through his backpack. The rest of us looked on incredulously as the gnome pulled out an extendable bipod and sniper rifle, setting it up on the side of the cruiser.

"What the hell have you got in there?" I asked.

"Always the right tools!" he said proudly. He looked over his shoulder at Alina. "Do you want to do the honors?"

She looked surprised, but took a seat behind the bipod and took the rifle in her hands. Having seen her sports bar and pitching ability, it was easy to forget that she had been a soldier.

"You don't have to do this," I said gently. Throwing baseballs and beer glasses in self-defense was one thing. Doing the job of an assassin was another.

"No problem," Gloric said, catching my meaning before the half-auric could reply. "Oxidium-based tranquilizer. No dirty cleanup!"

That made me breathe a little more easily. I already had a lot on my conscience for getting my new companions involved in the first place, and Tribe's impending torture weighed heavily. I didn't need to add murder to the tally.

Two figures stood on the NIGHT cruiser, silhouetted against the bright lights of Alcatraz. They walked back and forth on the little boat, stopping intermittently. Alina looked through the rifle's holoscope, steadying herself against the bobbing gunwale. They would neither of them be easy shots from a stable surface, let alone from the moving water cruiser.

The half auric exhaled slowly through her nose, then pulled the trigger. One of the silhouettes straightened, clutching its neck, then slumped out of sight.

Without hesitation, Alina cocked the sniper rifle, setting another tranq bullet in its chamber. The other shadow stood still for a moment, then ran over to the first, stooping out of view beneath the cruiser's side rim. The Pitcher waited patiently, picking her moment carefully. Within a few seconds, the figure raised its head to look around, and Alina squeezed the trigger again. The silhouette dropped.

"Nice shot," Vasshka offered.

"Thanks." Alina wiped her palms on her jeans and helped Gloric put the rifle away.

I steered the water cruiser over to the liberated vehicle, careful to keep the NIGHT cruiser in between us and the island's security floodlights, which illuminated everything within a half-mile of the headquarters. We sidled up next to the boat, using a loose metal board and some rope Vasshka found in the water cruiser to create a makeshift boarding plank. Alina climbed across it nimbly, fastening it more securely on the NIGHT vessel and then helping Buster and Gloric to join her.

I stood behind Doubleshot, who eyed the plank dubiously, pawing at her hat.

"Problem?" I asked.

"I can't swim," she said. It was the first time I had seen her nervous.

"You'll be fine," I assured her, hiding a smile.

The dwarf put a foot hesitantly on the board, using her hands to steady her. Gaining in confidence, she stood upright, putting her other foot forward.

Her timing could not have been worse. A large wave rippled underneath the cruisers, rocking strongly enough to separate them from one another by about a foot. The plank and rope held on the NIGHT vehicle, but dislodged from ours, dumping Doubleshot unceremoniously into the black water.

"Vasshka!" Gloric cried from the NIGHT cruiser.

"Piss," I cursed, stripping off my coat and shoes, tossing them to the other vehicle and diving overboard in the dwarf's direction.

The water was freezing, shocking my system and threatening to stop my heart for a few seconds. I kept my eyes closed, knowing that the salt water would do a number on my lenses, and instead moved my arms around wildly, searching. I brushed Vasshka's leather jacket almost immediately, and clasped it with my hand, feeling her weight pull me downwards. She was sinking like a stone.

I kicked my legs furiously, using my free hand to pull us to the surface and shifting so that I could grab the dwarf underneath her arms. She sputtered as we reappeared above water, and I looked up just in time to see Buster barrel into the water on top of us. The wolf had evidently seen the action and jumped in unnecessarily.

Alina threw me a rope and I used it to haul Vasshka to the NIGHT cruiser, inelegantly pushing on her bottom to help her lift herself onboard. I swam over to collect Buster, who was paddling happily in the frigid water, and guided him onto the hanging plank. Gloric grabbed the wolf's front paws, heaving as best as he could, and was rewarded by being trounced by a hundred-odd pounds of wet hound.

I clasped the rope and started climbing, then heard Vasshka's voice from overhead.

"My hat!" she protested.

I looked back in the water to see the dwarf's wide-brimmed hat floating peacefully among the waves. Sighing from the very core of my being, I swam back to grab it, feeling the chill pervade my bones.

Hat in tow, I pulled myself up the rope and onto the cruiser, collapsing on the metal deck. Vasshka lay in a heap next to me, her face ruddier than normal and her hair a tangled orange mess. Gloric hovered nearby, clucking over her, and Alina busied herself with putting away the ropes and plank.

The dwarf looked over at me pointedly, her horns glaring menacingly in the moonlight. "If you tell anyone about this..." she began.

I handed over her hat and forestalled any further comment. "Scout's honor," I promised.

Buster padded over and shook himself dry, spraying the three of us with cool Bay water. Vasshka sat up, complaining uncharacteristically about the hound, and put on her now floppy hat, which squished weirdly on her wet head. If I hadn't already been concerned that she would kill us all for witnessing her ignominy, I would have laughed. She looked ridiculous.

"We've got company," Alina called from the cruiser's little steering cabin.

I picked myself up, squeezing water from my shirt and pants and retrieving my shoes and coat from the floor. The dwarf and I had landed not far from the two tranquilized guards, a man and woman, who slept peacefully on the aft deck. I rummaged through their pockets, grabbing their digitabs.

I tossed the devices to Gloric as I made my way to the cabin. "Unlock these?" I requested, picking my steps carefully so as to not slip on my wet feet.

The steering cabin was a simple, unfurnished room with digital controls for the cruiser's engine and abovewater artillery. A narrow set of lockers stuck out from the rear wall, and various boxes filled with nautical tools sat neatly, riveted to the floor.

"What?" I asked, walking briskly to open an unmarked locker.

"One cruiser incoming, and a timed security check from the dispatcher," Alina explained, looking at several blinking messages on the central console.

The locker was empty, and I checked the next one, finding two bundles of neatly-pressed uniforms. Agents always kept extra clothes on the water-based vessels.

"Here, put these on," I said, handing Alina a set and beginning to strip off my wet clothes.

The half-auric eyed me curiously as I took off my shirt, and I was suddenly self-conscious in the cold air. She smiled enigmatically and turned away from me, undressing.

I did my damnedest to keep my eyes to myself, but I'd be lying if I said I didn't catch a flash of tanned skin and a few scars here and there. I made a promise to myself that the next time I was naked with someone from the opposite sex, it would not be on a boat with our lives at stake in the middle of the apocalypse.

I was grateful for the dry set of clothes, which were a little tight but serviceable. Alina's uniform was baggy on her slim body, but it would do. I would be recognizable by other agents on sight and the half-auric's disguise wouldn't stand up to any real scrutiny, but I hoped that our outfits would at least provide some cover from a distance.

Gloric's skills and whatever help we could garner from Madge would get us into the facility, but there were some limits to what they could do. Masking the image of a random water cruiser coming in to dock was one of them, which is why we needed the NIGHT vessel. Gloric could have disabled the perimeter camera systems, but that would create undue suspicion and likely result in more patrols being sent out to investigate.

The gnome walked into the cabin, empty-handed. I raised an eyebrow at him.

"Got their tabs?" I asked, running my hands through my hair to try to get some of the water out.

"Better," he said. "I've created micro-profiles on the network and synced them with yours. You should be able to use your own digitabs, with increased access levels."

I marveled at the technomancer's genius. "You're the best."

Gloric gave me a thumbs-up and returned amidships.

"ID requests from the cruiser and dispatcher have come in again," Alina said, looking at the console. The holodisplay's LEDs bathed her angular face in a soft green light.

I walked over to the console, pulling out my digitab and opening the micro-profile Gloric had set up for me. Sure enough, the male guard's information and access codes popped up, and I synced the identification protocol with the vessel's computer system, showing Alina how to do the same. I could see the other cruiser off our starboard prow, making its way slowly towards us.

The console beeped, accepting the verification, but the NIGHT cruiser kept moving in our direction. A button flashed in the holodisplay, indicating an incoming call.

I activated the call's audio. "Perimeter NVC two zero eight one, reporting," I said, using the vehicle's identification number.

"Two zero eight one, this is three six one niner," a female voice came through the console. "Please explain your delay in ID verification."

"Problem with the verification protocol, sir," I said, thinking on my feet. "It's been fixed."

There was a short pause, and I felt as though I could hear the other cruiser thinking.

"Please put on the vessel's commanding officer," the voice said at length.

I made a face at Alina, nodding at her digitab. She brought up the female guard's micro-profile and took over the call.

"First Lieutenant Talia Watson, reporting," the Pitcher said confidently.

"Lieutenant Watson, please provide vocal identification to confirm digital ID," the voice responded.

I fought down my panic, helping Alina to find the guard's identification number in the micro-profile. The cruiser's forelights continued to drift inexorably in our direction.

"Three six one niner, vocal identification is romeo, victor, zero, yankee, zero, delta, zero," Alina said with no hint of hesitation.

There was another pause as the cruiser checked her credentials. I held my breath.

"Carry on, two zero eight one," the voice replied.

I dropped the call, letting out a long breath. Alina and I shared a look of relief as the other cruiser's lights slowly turned away from our direction.

"Can you drive one of these things?" I asked her, lacing my boots.

"Think so."

I gave Alina an outline of the NIGHT headquarters' structure, directing her towards the facility's east-facing rear entrance. She pulled the cruiser around and started heading in that direction.

I made a quick call to Madge, who picked up after a short delay.

"Nightpath?" she said, using my title to let me know she was in mixed company.

"Madge, we're coming in pretty hot," I said. "I need you to find a reason for the camera crew to leave their posts. Five minutes, tops." I was fairly certain Gloric could handle the digital access we would need, while Alina and I took out any guards. Most of the Nightpaths, Daypaths, and Inquisitors would be in the middle of the fighting, hopefully leaving only a few that we would need to avoid. We would have to pass several visual security checkpoints, though, and it would be impossible for Alina and I to get through without a fight.

"OK," she said after a long pause, her voice distant. I had a sudden, irrational fear that she was still in Cuba, fighting in the city, or otherwise unable to help us.

Her hesitation worried me. "Madge, are we good?"

Silence.

I checked my digitab to make sure she was still on the call.

"Madge?"

"Everything's good, Nightpath," she said, more clearly. "I'll wait for your signal."

The line clicked, and I felt my eyes narrow in suspicion. I had realized that our plan depended on Madge's inside help, and trusted her implicitly. We had known each other since we were teenagers, and been through more things together than any two agents should have to. It hadn't crossed my mind that she might renege on helping us, or worse, give us away to Karthax. I liked to think that our bond was stronger than whatever sense of loyalty we had to the NIGHT leadership, but the past two days had given me plenty of reasons to doubt everything.

I pushed the thoughts out of my mind, dismissing them. Either Madge would help us, or she wouldn't. We didn't have much choice other than to keep moving.

I went to check on the others as Alina steered us within the island's security floodlights. Vasshka had stripped off her leather outer clothes and was standing in the middle of the deck in trousers and a black tank top, still dripping. Buster had his hands on the gunwale, taking in the ocean breeze, and Gloric was tapping at his portable keyboard, his eyes flitting from his glasses' display to that of his single-eye visor.

"I can see if there are some other clothes..." I offered to the dwarf.

"I'll live," she said, taking out a soggy cigar and trying to light it.

"You guys should be good up to the VPen," Gloric said, referring to the third underground level of the island fortress. "Anything lower will require a physical keycard as well as the digital security passes."

I nodded, already knowing the layout intimately. My own keycard would ordinarily be able to grant us entrance, but Karthax would have been sure to have had its access revoked. Even if he hadn't, use of the keycard would alert mission control of its user's presence, which would initiate all kinds of alerts. The NIGHT headquarters at large thought me dead, and would presume that anyone using my keycard was trying to break into the facility. They wouldn't be wrong.

I helped my companions get situated in a little maintenance area below deck, storing the sleeping guards with them. They were to wait for the five or so minutes that it would take for us to get into the facility, then take the cruiser north around the island and west towards the Embarcadero, drawing as much attention away from us as they could.

"How are you going to get out?" Gloric had asked as I told him my plan.

"Send me a helicarrier," I joked.

He looked at me straight, completely deadpan.

"Do *not* send me a helicarrier," I explained.

Alina came back to meet us as we neared the island's perimeter, wishing the others well. She knelt down to ruffle Buster's soft hair between his ears.

"Take care of them, buddy," she said quietly. The wolf licked her palm, whining softly.

I squatted next to her in the small space. "They'll be fine," I reassured her, uncertain.

We closed the hatch on the maintenance shaft, and I brought Gloric's visor camera up on a corner of my lens display. The gnome had connected all of our digitabs' communications systems and synced my video capture with his. What he saw, I would see, and vice-versa. Right now, I could only see the shadowed outlines of Doubleshot and Buster, with Gloric's hand typing away at the portable keyboard.

Alina and I returned to the cabin, and we both looked up at the approaching fortress. The island had always been imposing; historical photos would show its functionally minimalist buildings and solitary lighthouse squatting territorially atop the small mounds of dirt and scrub. In the modern era, it had been turned into something that looked like it was plucked from an Arthurian legend. Three white towers capped by circular turrets formed a triangle at the apexes of the island, surrounding the central structure, which had been rebuilt above and below ground. Smaller spires poked up from angular white buildings, gleaming with a fey light in the darkness.

I felt my heart quicken as we entered the dock perimeter, a long pair of piers crossed by a breakwater and protected by a retractable gate, which stood closed. Our plan would live or die by our ability to operate the gate.

Alina slowed the cruiser, decelerating as we entered the piers and letting the vehicle drift up to the gate. A lone guard was visible in the small building adjacent to the entrance. I used the console to hail the guardhouse, indicating to Alina that she should do the talking.

"NVC two zero eight one, you're not scheduled to return from patrol for another thirty minutes," the guard said through our console.

The Pitcher cleared her throat. "Orders to return to headquarters by Daypath Marguerite Liu," she said, giving Talia Watson's identification code again.

I could see Gloric's little fingers typing away furiously in my lenses' video frame, linking Madge's security clearance with some bogus return request. The gnome would take control of the gate himself when he, Vasshka, and Buster made their move, but we couldn't contend with the added attention at the moment.

"Clear to proceed," the guard said at length. The gate moved slowly apart with a mechanical whir, giving us entry to the island proper. I waved at the guard house as Alina maneuvered further between the piers, and saw the outline of a person waving back.

The piers continued for a short distance, leading to several other docks that were mostly empty for the time being. A few light and heavy cruisers floated here and there, but the majority were out in service of the city battle. Five guards were visible in front of the facility's rear entrance, two large reinforced doors that led directly into the base of the main building and underground.

The Pitcher cruised us into an empty space and turned off the engine. I grabbed a ceridium capsule and made sure my weapons, although damp, were ready.

"Wait here," I said to Alina, and used the capsule to create a shadow shroud. There was no way that our disguises would hold up to visual identification among the guards, so I would have to do it the old-fashioned way.

I crept out of the cruiser and onto the dock, a shadow against the dark pier. Several lights illuminated the area at regular intervals, but I clung to the darkness and quickly reached the cement platform that led to the entryway. Crouching behind a stone railing, I sent a message to Madge, hoping that she was able to give the camera crew something to do for five minutes or more.

"I'm going," I breathed, seeing the air in front of me turn to frost. It was considerably cooler out in the middle of the Bay.

"Starting the timer," I heard Gloric's voice, and saw his camera shift as he tinkered with his backpack.

Two of the guards stood close to me, on either side of the centermost ledge that led to the piers. Another two flanked the entryway, with the extra guard pacing interminably up the central path and back to the doors. All of them were visibly armed, their ceridium assault rifles strapped across their shoulders and chests.

I reached down over the platform, grabbing some loose soil from the ground beneath and placing it in my pocket. I then pulled a couple of tranq needles from my wrist pouch, placing them lengthwise in the grooves of my palms in between my first and middle fingers.

"No one gets killed," I remembered cautioning the group as we put together our plan coming back from Reno. "They're all just trying to do their jobs."

"You know what I do, right?" Vasshka had said through the speaker system.

"We'll get you some non-lethal bullets," I conceded. We hadn't. I wasn't sure how that was going to work out.

I waited for the patrol make her way onto the pier, then vaulted myself over the stone railing behind the platform guards, who were facing the ocean and away from the building. I landed silently in plain view of the man and woman guarding the entrance, their backs against the stone wall.

What they saw in that moment would have chilled most people to their core, bringing their darkest nightmares of murderous shadows to life. These two were seasoned guards in the NIGHT corps, used to seeing all manner of magic at the service of Nightpaths, Daypaths, and Inquisitors. They squinted in the fluorescent light, confused.

If they had put together any cogent thoughts about my appearance, they did not have time to voice them. I stood from my crouch and fanned my hands outwards, flinging the needles in their direction. The one on the right clutched his neck, and the left, her cheek. They both slumped to the floor, the night wind and distance muffling the sound considerably, but unable to block out the clattering of their weapons.

One of the platform guards began to turn, alarmed by the clamor. I closed the distance in an instant, spinning to gain momentum and leaving the ground. My boot met his jaw with a crunch, and he tumbled over the platform's railing and onto the dirt below. I bent my knees to cushion my landing, stepping in the direction of the other guard and thrusting my hand in my pocket.

He looked at me and his jaw began to drop, eyes widening. I tossed the dirt from my pocket at his face, preempting any sound or scream. I moved swiftly around him to place my arms around his neck in a three-pointed choke, dragging him out of the light and away from the platform. He struggled against my grip but soon relaxed, unconscious. I turned his head to the side to make certain he wasn't going to swallow any more dirt, and pressed myself back against the stone railing.

The patrol finished her round, walking back towards the platform. Halfway up the gangway, she noticed the prone forms of the other guards, and turned her walk into a run, holding her rifle in one hand and reaching for her digitab with the other. She would press a button and sound an alert, bringing more guards on top of my head.

I didn't give her the opportunity. I drew my stunner and steadied it against the railing in one swift motion, firing an electrified round at her moving profile. It wasn't my best shot, and hit the reinforced padding of her uniform, startling her but not attaching to her skin. She turned around, looking for me, and grabbing again for her digitab.

A bolt appeared from nowhere, sticking like a dart in between her nose and lip. Her eyes rolled back in her head and she wavered, falling back against the railing and then forward to lie on her face.

I looked in the direction of the NIGHT cruiser to see Alina standing behind the prow, still looking down the holoscope of the sniper rifle in her hands. She held the position for a moment, and then looked over the weapon at me, raising a hand.

"Thanks," I said. I spoke a word and dispelled my shadow shroud, returning the gesture.

"Ayup," her voice said into my earpiece.

I waited for the half-auric to put away the sniper rifle, idly watching Gloric type. Alina joined me after a moment, and we walked towards the building.

"Hope these things work," she said, pulling up the NIGHT cruiser guard's stolen profile on her digitab.

"They'll work," Gloric's voice reverberated in our ears.

We walked up to the entrance, using our digitabs to verify our clearance to enter. They worked without a hitch, silently swinging the reinforced doors outwards.

"Hold up," I said as the Pitcher took a step forward.

I bent and grabbed the door guards' simple caps, offering one to Alina and putting on the other.

"Keep your hat low and eyes forward," I instructed. "And walk like you own the place."

There would be a small number of personnel about, officials and staff mostly, with the lion's share of combat-ready agents on the front lines. No one would question two guards on their way through the facility, particularly if their access codes checked out. It was unlikely that anyone would notice the sleeping guards outside before the camera crew came back online, giving us about four minutes to reach Tribe and locate the data drive.

I looked up at the line of holocameras overhead as we strode through the doors, hoping against hope that Madge had been able to do her magic, and that we wouldn't run into any other agents on our way. I wouldn't know whether to fight or reason with them, and either option would take too much time.

The NIGHT facility was exactly as I had remembered it, plain whitewashed walls with simple blackened chrome trims along the baseboards and door frames. Digital notices scrolled automatically in holodisplay monitors recessed within the walls, all currently projecting location information about the impending war. The air smelled like paint and rubber shoe soles, with the faint metallic aroma of ceridium weaponry. I felt a strange sense of cognitive dissonance, a homecoming in someone else's house.

The area we had stepped into was a secondary checkpoint, a short hallway that opened up into a larger room with a square booth in the middle. Reinforced glass walls that blocked entry and exit flanked the kiosk, uninterrupted save a door panel that had been cut into either side. The booth itself was concrete up to waist level, and glass all the way to the ceiling. A guard sat behind a desk in the kiosk, watching a holodisplay report on the state of the battle.

"Karen," I said under my breath to Alina, recognizing the guard.

We walked up to the entrance wall, using the stolen profiles to verify our identities against a freestanding console next to the door. The computer beeped in authentication, waiting on the guard to provide confirmation.

The guard, absorbed in the report, pressed a button without looking at us. The door slid open against the glass wall, and we walked briskly through.

"Thanks, Karen," Alina mumbled, keeping her head forward.

"Yeah," the guard said, ignoring us.

We did our best to keep our pace normal, striding down the hallway past the checkpoint and into a large reception area with several passageways leading off in different directions. Two booths protruded from the left-hand wall, housing a number of dispatchers who were busily coordinating responses to assaults around the city. I raised my hand to scratch at my face, trying to prevent anyone from giving up my cover.

I needn't have worried. The dispatchers paid us no mind, and the place was otherwise deserted. I took us through the centermost hallway, quickening our walking speed as we passed room after empty room, coming eventually to the large central concourse of the facility.

The Gressler Atrium, named after the first Inquisitor General, was not-so-mute testament to the seat of NIGHT power. A white stone dome one hundred feet across hovered protectively overhead, concentric circles of reinforced glass giving glimpses of the night sky above and relieving some of the oppressiveness. Banks of metal chairs sat bolted into the marble tiled floor, glittering under the fluorescent lighting. Potted ferns and other plants were scattered about the room, giving some color to the otherwise minimalist room, and four enormous monitors filled the walls on the ordinal directions of the atrium, displaying information about agent shifts, battle updates, and other reports.

Free-standing consoles stood about the room at regular intervals, available for agents and visitors who had need of accessing network functions not provided through a digitab. Having entered the atrium through the east corridor, we stood next to a few vending machines that glowed with AR displays of different foods and soft drinks. Another hallway opened across the concourse from us and to the left and right on the cardinal directions, and rows of framed pictures and honors lined the walls beneath the monitors and in between the hallways.

I heard Alina catch her breath next to me, and understood her emotions at that moment. The Gressler Atrium captured the NIGHT ethos perfectly in its architecture; it was spartan and imposing while still being technologically modern. Its creators had spared no expense in its construction, and it had a dark beauty in its simplicity. Although pictures of it were used in most media propaganda related to NIGHT activity, they were no substitute for seeing the facility in person for the first time.

The room felt cold and sterile to me, a monument to the government's willingness to spend countless funds on technological advancement to support a primeval xenophobia. I can't say that I'd ever put too much thought into what the NIGHT leadership stood for, beyond some vague discomfort at my own involvement in whatever underrace oppression resulted from our activity. I normally viewed the world in more simple terms, applying my skills where necessary to keep the city safe from revolutionary terrorism.

The Destroyer's words about the status quo nagged at me, disturbing me more than I'd liked to admit. I was no longer sure who needed to be kept safe from whom.

"Three minutes, folks," Gloric spoke into our earpieces. I could see him and Vasshka preparing to leave the NIGHT cruiser's storage compartment.

I led Alina swiftly into the atrium, keeping a low profile as we skirted the northeastern wall. The room was quiet, with only a couple of night shift workers cleaning the area and a some off-duty officials occupying a cluster of chairs, watching the reports on one of the monitors. We followed the curvature of the wall to the nearest hallway, passing by several framed pictures of the Inquisitor Generals, from Gressler all the way to Karthax.

Just as we reached the north entrance, a squad of agents came bustling through, their combat boots clicking on the marble floor. An Inquisitor led the group, speaking instructions over her shoulder to three Daypaths and one Nightpath. They crossed directly in front of us, turning in our direction to take the east exit.

I quickly spun Alina towards a nearby console, fiddling with my digitab and coughing to cover my face. The Pitcher reached up casually to adjust her hat, keeping her back to the advancing agents. I could hear brief bits of the Inquisitor's orders to her subordinates as they passed behind us, instantly recognizing the names and ranks I heard. I felt a conflicting set of emotions, camaraderie and familiarity warring with anger and vengeance. I had to remind myself that none save a few of my former comrades would have had anything to do with Karthax's betrayal and my attempted assassinations.

The agents exited through the eastern door, and Alina and I continued along the wall past the north entryway and into the western one. A hall identical to the one through which we had come led away from the atrium and into another maze of corridors, but we took an immediate right to a set of huge elevators that led up into one of the headquarters' three towers, and down into the bowels of the island. I used my digitab's stolen profile to activate one of the elevators, Gloric's enhanced access codes giving us clearance.

"Five agents coming your way," I said to the gnome, who had taken the helm of the NIGHT cruiser and was preparing to steer it out of the harbor.

"We'll get a move on," Vasshka replied for him as the technomancer starting the engine, still typing.

The elevator opened with a chime, empty. I said a silent thank-you and we stepped inside, taking it to the third belowground level, which housed the VPen subject rooms. My stomach flew into my chest as the high-speed elevator took us into the earth, opening a moment later into a small antechamber.

If the upper levels of the facility seemed cold, the VPen was an unemotional wasteland in comparison. Concrete walls and ceilings pressed in claustrophobically, a reminder of the hundreds of tons of building and rock above and around us. A reinforced glass and metal entryway was the only concession to the basic stonework, along with a simple linoleum floor. A security console stood next to the VPen's entrance, but the adjacent guard booth was empty.

"The hell?" I said out loud.

"Problem?" Alina asked, looking through the glass at the cells beyond.

I shook my head, perplexed. Even with the war going on outside, there should be at least one on-duty guard in attendance at all hours. I looked up at a security camera to our right, wondering if Madge had also cleared the checkpoint to help us.

"Gloric," I said, "Can you get me a read on Tribe's cell number?"

"Kind of busy here," the technomancer announced, steering the cruiser in between the piers. He would have to override the gate's security to get out of the island's perimeter, which would alert the gate guard and start the chain reaction that would send the NIGHTs' remaining forces after them and away from us. They would hopefully assume that the gnome was responsible for the unconscious guards, who would be spotted at any minute by the camera crew or the group of agents we had passed. Still, he was able to pull up information about the VPen's layout and give us a cell number.

"Fifty-one C," he said. I could see the eastern gate swing open in front of them, the Bay cold and dark ahead.

"Thanks." We used our digitabs to gain entry to the VPen, passing through the security wall and making a beeline for Tribe's cell.

The VPen subject cells were no more than adjacent rooms built into small concrete bunkers within a larger, open air worked stone cavern. Each room was affixed with a metal, digitally-operated door and would have basic living accoutrements within. The VPen's inhabitants would spend most of their waking hours with their headsets enabled, enduring whatever virtual punishment their sentence required, and given breaks for exercise, sleep, and some personal time. Tribe's cell was in one of the larger sections, which made me suspect that they had him locked up with other revolutionary interrogees.

We found the room without incident, and I used my digitab to disable its security system. The locking mechanism beeped, echoing hollowly in the silent cavern. The only other sound I could hear was Alina's breathing, and a distant alarm through Gloric and Vasshka's microphones as my companions left the island behind them.

I slid open the door, letting my eyes adjust to the darkness in front of me and relying on my lenses to tell me the rest. Two chairs sat back to back in the middle of the room, their occupants fastened in place with security clasps. Tribe's form was clearly visible even without my lenses, his head resting low over his chest and his hair hanging stringily over a VPen visor. Several pieces of basic furniture framed the room, with a simple washing station and toilet in the corner.

"Tribe," Alina breathed, seeing the auric's miserable shape. She pushed past me to rush to his side, and I followed her into the room.

I saw a flash of movement to my right, and spun to intercept it, a fraction too late. The butt of a ceridium spear connected with my jaw, sending me sprawling over a small food table and past Tribe's chair onto the floor. I heard a commotion, followed by Alina's yell, cut short by the thud of metal on bone. With no small effort, I rolled painfully onto my back, but the room refused to come into focus.

Through my lenses' augmented vision, I could see the Destroyer's red and white form stalking towards me, his staff rippling with blue fire. I scrambled to rise to my feet but he planted his foot in my chest, setting the tip of the spear against my throat. Behind him, I saw Alina propping herself up feebly alongside the chair behind Tribe's, its occupant clearly visible from my location. Madge slouched against her security clasps, her slim face streaked with blood and a VPen visor resting on her forehead.

A small, conscious place in my hazy mind screamed as it put the pieces together just as another tall figure entered the room, black and grey combat fatigues blending in with the walls under a black beret. I struggled feebly against the entromancer's boot, feeling the spear prick my skin and blood trickle down my neck.

"Welcome back, Nightpath," Karthax said from the doorway.

TEN

The VPen? It is absolutely safe. We have taken the utmost precaution to ensure that its detainees are treated with respect and care.
  -William D. Karthax, NIGHT Inquisitor General

I forced myself to focus, taking as deep of breaths as the auric's foot and spear would allow. A profound silence stretched in the room as time stood still, broken only by the sound of my shallow breaths and Tribe mumbling in a low voice. I blinked, seeing Vasshka on the deck of the NIGHT cruiser in Gloric's vision, drawing her pistols with Buster in tow. I could vaguely hear the gnome yelling something in my ear.

Karthax stood in the doorway for a moment, a statue in the dim light. I allowed my eyes to settle on him, using his hard features as a lifeline to help reel in my vision. The Inquisitor General epitomized the image of the grizzled veteran, his craggy face clean-shaven and stonelike under thin grey eyebrows. He had broad shoulders and a thick frame that would have seemed stocky but for his soldier's posture and bearing. His irises, silver even in the dark room, were mechanical, a hawk's eyes surveying the field below.

He walked into the room, flicking casually with one hand, and the assassin removed the spear from my neck. With a surge of energy, I barreled through my daze and grabbed at the Destroyer's boot, twisting it from my chest and reaching for my weapons.

The auric was faster than lightning. He shifted his hips and struck me in the side of the head with the flat of the spear's blade. I fell painfully on my bruised ribs, sprawled at Karthax's feet.

"Predictable," he said disapprovingly, squatting down next to me. I reached out feebly against his high-laced boots, and received a kick in the stomach from the Destroyer for my efforts. I began coughing uncontrollably, feeling my ribs pulse in agony.

Karthax watched me sputter, then shook his head. "Finish it," he said, getting up to leave.

The dark room was black with pain, and I felt myself slipping into the waiting embrace of unconsciousness. The tiniest, most remote part of my mind knew that if I passed out, my life was forfeit, as well as those of my friends and most of the city. I focused on the pain, holding onto it as though my very existence depended on it.

"Why," I hacked at Karthax's receding form.

Karthax stopped, turning back to face me. "What?"

I coughed several times, feeling strength returning to my voice through the pain. "Why are you doing this?"

The Inquisitor General stood watching me, towering in his fatigues. He walked over to me, crouching again.

"You were a good agent," he said quietly, misunderstanding my question. "But war requires certain concessions. It's nothing personal."

"No," I protested, tasting blood in my mouth. "Why does Thog'run get the city?"

Karthax paused, watching my face carefully. His cold eyes bored into me, searching. I could feel the Destroyer's spear poised, hovering above me.

"Nonhumans never cease to amaze me," the Inquisitor General said eventually. "Always focusing on the present moment, without looking at the bigger picture."

He played with a ceridium ring on his right hand, rolling it around his finger. "It was child's play to find you and your comrades, if they can be called that," he continued. "You were too focused on what was in front of your nose, ignoring everything else around you."

"You lured us here," I reasoned, trying to push myself up on one arm. The entromancer jabbed me in the side with his spear as a warning.

Karthax nodded, looking over at Tribe and Madge. "The coercion of Daypath Liu saddens me greatly, but it was necessary to bring you in. We cannot risk exposure, at this time or any. The thief will be useful, however."

I furrowed my brow, confused, but tried a different tact. "You're willing to sacrifice innocent lives for the sake of peace?"

The Inquisitor General continued to stare at me, unreadable. If I had touched any sort of emotion within him, it didn't show. I could have gleaned more information from the concrete walls.

"The world doesn't want peace," he said dismissively. "It wants security. I am here to make certain that it gets it, nothing more."

The human rose again to leave, nodding curtly at the assassin.

"Project Watershed!" I yelled at his back, desperately trying to keep his attention.

Karthax stopped, turning slowly. "That gnome of yours is quite the liability, with everything he has told you," he said mechanically. "We'll have him neutralized in no time."

I took the briefest of moments to focus on Gloric's vision in my lens display. He and the others seemed to be racing west towards the Embarcadero, engaged in a firefight with one or more water cruisers.

Something Karthax had said sparked a thought in my mind, and I decided to press it. "The bigger picture," I said up to him, half reasoning, half bluffing. "You don't intend to give Thog'run the city at all."

The man's eyes crinkled slightly in what could have been a smile. "Your logic befits the human part of you," he said. "Or did the Sigil give that away?"

I shook my head vigorously. It hurt. "I know all about it," I bluffed. "The auric king, the protected data drive, the innocents in the Oxidium dispensary..."

The Inquisitor General strode briskly towards me, kicking me in the face. I tried to roll away from him to ease the blow, but my nose and cheek exploded in pain.

"You know nothing," Karthax hissed, his eyes glowing fiercely and silver fire coalescing at his fingertips. I had hit a nerve.

"The auric king-" I pressed.

"You're all the same," he spat. "There's no such thing as an innocent addict. Thog'run is no different, and his people will pay the price of his insolence."

I coughed again, blinking away blood. "Thog'run's people," I said dumbly, my hazy mind picking up the pieces he was putting down but unable to put them together. I kept pressing. "You're going to let Thog'run take the city…"

"A temporary setback."

"…because you're going to kill his people."

He nodded, regaining his composure somewhat. "With the very thing they depend upon."

Oxidium. Karthax was going to concede the city to the revolutionaries, only to wipe them out with the drug. They had eluded the NIGHTs for so long, but once Karthax had them out in the open, the Inquisitor General could turn them all into ragers wholesale. Bigger picture, without a doubt.

I looked at the entromancer, who was ready to spear me like a wild boar. "And you, Agrid the Destroyer?" I was grasping at straws, and knew it. "You're going to let this happen to your own?"

The auric snorted, his pale skin ghastly and burning eyes measured. A pink crescent ringing his temple was the only sign of injury from our previous altercation. "I chose my allegiances a long time ago, half-human. Do not think to sway me."

I tried to remain calm. "They'll figure it out," I said weakly.

"Perhaps," Karthax said coolly, "but the city will be once again under our control by then."

I thought through the possible scenarios, my deductive reasoning working about as well as a train through sludge. Karthax's plan to triple-cross the auric king depended on his ability to contaminate the revs and most all of the underraces in San Francisco with Oxidium. That meant a bomb or some other way of distributing the drug over the fifty or so square miles of the city. It eluded me.

I tried to keep him talking. "Other people know about the data drive. They'll trace it back to you."

For once, Karthax looked confused. "Data drive?"

I didn't know how to respond, so I went with the truth. "The protected data drive, with details on Project Watershed. Secreted from the network."

His eyes narrowed as he took my meaning, then he laughed, once. It was not pleasant.

"What need have I for a data drive?" Karthax guffawed. Even the Destroyer chuckled.

I stared at him blankly, and he pointed meaningfully at his head.

"You're the data drive," I breathed, understanding. I felt my head slip back towards the floor in defeat. Our threadbare plan was starting to unravel completely.

"The nonhuman failing, Nightpath, is the inability to imagine that others think differently than you do. Unlike your people, I plan for the long haul. I wouldn't get very far if I left a data trail everywhere I went."

"No, but you left me," I said wearily. "And now you're tying up loose ends, so you can let the revs have their run of the city, and what? Set off an Oxidium bomb over San Francisco? Make everyone take the drug with their coffee?"

"Put it in their water," Alina's voice echoed from the nearby chairs. She had risen from the ground and was pointing her pistol at the Destroyer. "That's how I would do it."

She stood protectively near Tribe, unwavering even as blood streaked down her face. "Put down the spear," she said quietly, her voice low and dangerous.

"Kill him," Karthax ordered.

Several things happened at once. Two shots rang out as beside me, Karthax clapped his hands together, smashing the ceridium ring in between them. A bolt of silver fire escaped his clasped fingers, flashing across the room and flinging Alina against the opposing wall. She hit the concrete like a ragdoll and fell to the floor.

The Inquisitor General's spell wasn't quick enough to spoil her shot, however. Agrid the Destroyer had just enough time to twist away from the ceridium bullet, bending his body backwards and to the side.

The movement saved his life. A second bullet, aimed for his heart, hit him in the shoulder from the room's entrance. The auric faltered for a moment, clutching his arm and stumbling into a small table.

I looked up towards the doorway, relief pouring through my body as I saw the familiar face.

"Striker," I breathed.

"Hands where I can see them, both of you," the human said, holding his pistol expertly in front of him. His crew cut blond hair stood on end, and his normally flush face was tomato red from exertion. He looked like he had been running.

Karthax stood staring at the newcomer, unflinching. "Put the weapon down, Agent Johnson."

"No can do, boss," Striker said, his weapon still trained on the Destroyer. "Hands up or I finish the job."

"Put the weapon down," Karthax's voice was cool, unyielding. "I will not ask you again."

"No can do," Striker repeated. A single bead of sweat slid down his temple.

"Agent Johnson-" Karthax took a step towards him, perceptibly raising his voice.

Calmly, Striker shifted his aim towards the Inquisitor General and pulled the trigger. The bullet ripped through the human's fatigues, eating through whatever conventional armor he had on underneath and burning through his upper torso. Karthax stopped in his tracks, swaying on his feet and smashing into the wall adjacent to him.

The movement was all that Agrid the Destroyer needed. He made three quick motions with his uninjured hand, blowing air out of his nose and sucking in his tongue in succession. Striker turned to reorient his aim just as a pair of rhinoceros horns erupted from his chest. The human fell to his knees, dropping the pistol and clawing at the air. Blood bubbled from his mouth and his eyes widened in surprise.

The entromancer retracted his spear, stashing it in his maroon overcoat and pinning his injured arm to his chest. He strode over to Karthax, who was slowly sliding down the wall, leaving a crimson streak in his wake. I pushed myself up to my knees, painfully sluggish, and fumbled inside my coat for my pistol. I grabbed it, releasing it from its holster and pointing it at the Destroyer, but was far too slow. The auric spoke a word of power and he and Karthax disappeared, my bullet taking a chunk out of the concrete wall.

I sat on my knees for a minute, fighting down waves of pain and wiping blood away from my face. Slowly, I stumbled to my feet and staggered over to Striker, who was sitting ignominiously in the doorway, the magically-produced horns protruding from his chest. He was still breathing, faintly.

"You made it," I said, squatting next to him.

"Got your message," he said with a weak smile. His ruddy face had turned an ashen grey.

"Just hold on, buddy," I reassured him. "Alina is a healer-"

"No," he said with finality. "I don't want some knife-ears broad touching me in my privates."

"Racist," I offered.

He shook his head feebly. "Karthax is bad, man. Genocide and world domination. That's racist."

I nodded, saying nothing.

The human lifted a hand to grab my shirt, surprisingly strong.

"I did a bad thing, Nightpath," he said fervently.

"Make out with a dwarf?" I asked gently.

He shook his head again. "Worse," he replied laboriously, a little blood trickling from the corner of his mouth. "I didn't know what room your friend was in, so I kind of...opened all of them."

I shrugged. Even if the cell doors were deactivated, the VPen inhabitants would still be locked into their virtual simulations.

"Ragers, a lot of them," he explained, seeing my indifference. "Just locked up in their own piss."

That was bad. The NIGHTs would have no need to lock up victims of the rage plague in VPen chairs; no computer chip in the world would affect them when they were in their altered state.

"Where'd they come from?" I asked him, exhausted. It had been a long day, and the last thing I needed was a bunch of raving monsters tearing me and my companions limb from limb.

"I don't know. I saw some alchemancy-type stuff, looks like they were experimenting on them. Some of them were sedated, but others..."

An inhuman voice howled in the distance outside the room. I looked up at the sound, which echoed strangely against the concrete walls.

I turned back to the human, squeezing his hand. "You're a bastard, Striker."

"Don't I know it."

"Wait here," I said, hearing the ridiculousness of my comment as soon as it left my mouth.

I sheathed my pistol and hurried over to Alina, gingerly rolling her over and touching the side of her neck. I felt a pulse, slow but strong, and pulled several syringes of Oxadrenalthaline out of my coat. I applied a couple to my ribs and head first, feeling the drug erase the pain instantaneously, then held the half-auric in my lap and used another two needles on her face and back. The entromancer's spear had left a nasty gash under the Pitcher's eye, and Karthax's spell would have given her a few bruises, but nothing seemed broken.

Alina's skin warmed in my touch, and her eyes fluttered open after a few moments. She stared at me blindly for a second, then her eyes focused on my face.

"Did I get him?" she croaked, putting her hand on mine.

I smirked and shook my head, relieved by the sound of her voice. "No, but he did."

The half-auric followed my gaze to Striker, who was bleeding out on the floor. The sight gave her a jolt of energy, and she sat up quickly, using my arm to steady her.

"I'll see what I can do," she said, half-walking, half-crawling over to him.

I turned my attention to Tribe and Madge, still sitting in their simulations, oblivious to the world. I used my digitab to disable their VPen chips, then the security clasps keeping them in their chairs. They continued to sit there, mesmerized by whatever horrors they had been experiencing.

This close to him, I could hear Tribe repeating a rhyme from some unknown hip hop song, a litany that I hoped had kept him sane through the torture. I pulled the visor and headphones off of his head, untangling them from his sweaty hair. He stared into space, his lips still moving.

I let him readjust to the world and freed Madge from her VPen apparatus. Her olive shaped eyes rolled in her head as I took off the visor, then she shook herself and saw me. Our eyes met and she thrust herself forward in relief. I caught her and held her in my arms as she buried her face in my chest.

"Eskander," she sobbed. "They made me tell them where you were and when you were coming. I couldn't do anything, I'm sorry."

I shushed her gently, stroking her hair and trying to calm her. My heart ached for what they had put her through, but we didn't have much time before the ragers found us and Karthax's plan did more damage.

"We need to get out of here," I said as gently as I could. "Can you walk?"

She pulled away from me, tears streaking down her bloodied face. She nodded, and I saw her clamp down on her emotions with an effort. She wiped her face and nodded again, steel in her eyes.

"What's happening?" she asked.

I gave her a quick overview of the current situation, Karthax's triple-cross against the auric king, and the meager remnants of our own plan.

"Striker's down," I concluded, jerking my head over towards the fallen human, being tended to by Alina. "My friend's looking after him, but it's mortal. Can you counterspell?"

Madge pushed herself to her feet, steadying herself on the chair. She peered over my shoulder, then looked at me squarely, shaking her head once.

I cursed, vehemently. I had hoped her photomancy could at least dispel the Destroyer's magic.

"I've stopped his bleeding, but he's still got two horns sticking out of his chest," Alina said as she walked up to us. She extended a hand to Madge, introducing herself.

The Daypath took her hand, shaking it firmly. "Nice no-hitter in the sixty-two series."

"Thanks."

Madge turned her attention back towards Striker, who was staring back at us from under heavy eyelids. "I can put him in a stasis field..."

Several howls sounded not far from the opening of the cell, announcing the arrival of some newcomers. Whatever we were going to do, we would have to hurry.

"Do it, but quickly. Medical will look after him, but we have to get him there first."

Madge nodded. "Ceridium?"

I handed her a couple of capsules, and she walked over to Striker.

I pulled out my digitab, enabling the VPen's security system. The door slid closed with a hiss.

I looked at Tribe, who was still staring into space, his mouth working silently. Gently, I put my hand on his arm, shaking him softly.

"Hey, buddy," I said, allowing the slightest bit of urgency into my voice. "Time to go."

His eyes moved vaguely in my direction, focusing briefly and then glazing over again. I shook him a bit more strongly, and he sagged loosely in my grasp.

I set him back against the chair and rummaged through his clothing, finding without difficulty a small packet in one of his jacket's many pockets. Karthax had seen no need to strip him of his Oxidium, most likely preferring to fuel his addiction. I took one of the little tablets and dropped it on the auric's tongue, tipping his chin back and pinching his throat to get him to swallow.

The drug took hold within a matter of seconds, and Tribe lurched back into consciousness like a diver coming to the surface. He turned to the side and retched, throwing up the Oxidium and whatever paltry food the NIGHTs had given him. I grabbed a couple of towels from a nearby sink and handed one to him, pressing the other against my bloody face and trying to multitask. In the corner of my lens display, I could see Gloric's sight of the Embarcadero, his shorter perspective bobbing after Vasshka and Buster up a long pier. They had disembarked and were being pursued, the dwarf running backwards in Gloric's vision, firing at something behind them two at a time.

Tribe wiped his face fastidiously, shuddering a little as nightmares left his body. He dropped the towel and looked up to face me, a haunted look in his eyes.

"You hurt?" I asked perfunctorily, watching Vasshka guide the gnome and wolf into a waiting party of revolutionaries.

The auric shook his head, surveying the room. He noticed Alina and Madge in the corner, the Daypath casting a long spell, golden light escaping her fingertips and coating Striker's still form with brilliance.

"Who're they?" he said in a faraway voice.

"Friends."

He nodded listlessly, reaching a slender hand up to scratch his tangled hair. Ponderously, he reached into his pocket to pull out another Oxidium tablet, then thought better of it and put it away.

"Gloric," I said into my microphone, giving Tribe a little time to get his bearings.

The gnome's voice chimed cheerily in my earpiece. "You guys dead yet?" he panted, still running.

"Not on my watch," I quipped, pulling up a layout of the NIGHT headquarters on my digitab. "How's it going over there?"

"Never been better." The sounds of ceridium weapons and artillery filled the background. "Met up with some of Vasshka's friends, still trying to keep the heat off of you. The Embarcadero is a warzone!"

"I believe it." I flicked a finger over the digitab, flipping through the different levels of the facility until I reached the VPen. "Catch any of our conversation here?"

"You getting beat up while Karthax betrays the auric king?" Gloric's vision spun as he whirled, firing a pair of rockets from his shoulders at the mouth of an alleyway behind them. They each hit an opposing wall, crumbling them to block entry. "I heard it. What's the plan?"

"I'm trying to figure that out," I said, enlarging the image of the VPen to look at any alternate elevators. There weren't any, just a heavily fortified service staircase on the opposite side from the main entrance.

"What's happening here?" Alina asked as she and Madge walked over. Tribe and the Daypath took a long look at each other, and exchanged nods.

"Karthax and the Destroyer are escaping," I said, "and we've got an army of ragers and at least a handful of agents and security in between us and them."

"What's their deal?" Tribe asked distractedly, and I remembered that he hadn't been privy to the depth of the Inquisitor General's betrayal or my recap to Madge.

"The war is a setup," Alina explained, checking the thief for injuries. "Karthax is going to triple-cross the auric king, giving him the city but then poisoning all the underraces with Oxidium."

The auric perked up at that. "How?"

The Pitcher shrugged. "The water system is my best guess."

"I can confirm that," Gloric's voice rang into our earpieces. I put him and Vasshka on speakerphone so Madge and Tribe could hear him. "The Sigil's eyes have noticed some revolutionary movement away from the fighting and near the public utilities core. Must be the Destroyer's people."

I listened to the gnome, thinking. There was no way we could intercept the revolutionaries loyal to Karthax in time, and without the nonexistent data drive, we would only have my lens recordings as evidence to bring the Inquisitor General to justice. I wasn't confident that they would be enough.

"So, they're going to let Thog'run into the city, then kill him," Madge summed up.

I nodded. "Classic bait-and-switch. They'll give the auric king his run of San Francisco, and then poison his constituents with Oxidium until they tear themselves apart."

The Daypath stared at me stoically, but I could see the emotions roiling behind her brown eyes. She had worked for Karthax for a long time, and the betrayal would have hit her the hardest.

"We have to do something," Tribe announced suddenly, coming out of his reverie.

"We're doing it," I said placatingly. "I'll go after Karthax-"

"No, I mean right now," he pressed. "Thog'run will ride into the city himself, and there's no telling what else Karthax might have planned. If the Oxidium doesn't kill him, something or someone else will."

A steel shone in Tribe's eyes, unlike anything I had seen from the normally insouciant auric. Karthax's betrayal of Thog'run seemed to have bothered him.

"What do you know, Tribe?" I asked gently.

He looked at me intensely, his chest rising and falling slowly. The silence stretched awkwardly as we all watched him, waiting for his reply.

A shadow passed over his face as he searched mine, and his expression changed from defiant, to troubled, and back to his usual easygoing look. He seemed to be considering his words carefully.

"I know him," he said eventually.

"Since when?" Alina asked.

Tribe shook his head, his stringy hair sticking to his face. "Long time ago, when I first joined the movement. He helped me and my brother, long story. Before all of…"

He swept his hands towards himself. "…this."

I cleared my throat in the quiet that followed, interested in what the auric had to say but knowing we had precious little time to move. "Would he recognize you?"

"What?" he looked confused.

"Thog'run," I said insistently. "Would he know your face?"

"I…yes," the thief replied, looking at me like I had three heads. "Yes, he would."

I gambled. "Gloric," I spoke into my microphone, "get me the auric king."

ELEVEN

Thog'run II has taken his throne by force, but this does not indicate that he is unwanted as king. For who permits sovereignty but those who are to be subjects?

-The Sigil of Sparks

The gnome's vision bobbed as he trailed Doubleshot into a dark building, following the dwarf and her colleagues through a narrow corridor and down into an underground tunnel. It looked as though they were traveling through one of the revs' many subterraneous networks.

"I'm sorry, what?" Gloric puffed.

"Thog'run," I said impatiently. "Do you have a direct line to him, or not?"

The sound of shots being fired emanated through the digitab as the group encountered resistance in the tunnel. It seemed that the NIGHTs had anticipated their chosen route.

"Kind of busy here," the gnome groused for a second time, jumping off a makeshift ladder and into the tunnel. He wheeled to run behind a waiting group of revolutionaries, who were providing cover fire against the waylayers.

"It's important," I insisted, looking around at the little party in the VPen. "As in, *right now* important."

"Alright, alright, give me a second," he said, pulling out a keyboard as he ran.

"Can you do a splitscreen? Let him see what I see."

"Sure, just..." the gnome's little fingers typed furiously. "Hang on."

The display whirled as something knocked into Gloric, tumbling him to the side. Buster popped into view as the gnome righted himself, somehow holding onto his keyboard and seeing a ceridium mortar blast the spot in which he had just been standing. The technomancer returned a volley of his own, turning on his heel before seeing if his shot hit its mark.

"Sorry about that," he said, clicking buttons as he resumed running. A holodisplay emanated from his keyboard, and he tapped through several different interfaces, finally settling on one. "Got it!"

"Thanks," I remarked, waiting.

It took a couple of beeps, but then I was staring into the face of Thog'run II, King of Aurichome and leader of the revolutionaries, on his private display.

"What is the meaning of this?" he said in a deep, growling voice, his black, beady eyes narrowing at the sight of my face. The auric was on some open-air vehicle of sorts with a phalanx of soldiers on hovering motorcycles visible behind him, subsurface earthen walls racing past them.

"King Thog'run," I began, "my name is Eskander Aradowsi. Until recently, I have been employed as a Nightpath at the Pacific South NIGHT headquarters-"

"I know who you are," he snapped. "The agent who has eluded death to spoil the most secret of carefully-laid plans."

I took his comment as a complement. "Yes, well, those plans may not be turning out the way that you've intended."

The auric stared at me, his piglike nose jerking as though he could smell me through the digitab. His black hair, caught in long topknot, flew behind him as he rode through the underground.

"What have you done?" he said, his tone like that of a father admonishing a wayward child.

"Not me. Karthax," I explained. "He's not going to hold up his end of the bargain. You'll find several of your forces loyal to him preparing to poison the city's water system with Oxidium. San Francisco will be yours, but it will be full of ragers in no time."

The auric didn't miss a beat. "How do you know this, half-human?"

"Karthax told me himself, while he was trying to kill me. Check your people near the public utilities core, and you'll have more than enough proof. And if you don't believe me," I lifted my digitab in front of my face to capture Tribe in my vision, which would display him on Thog'run's screen. "Ask him."

Thog'run's brow furrowed as he took in the sight of the thief sitting in his VPen chair, disheveled and dirty but confident. For his part, Tribe met my gaze as though he was looking into the auric king's eyes, and his demeanor changed. His posture straightened, and he somehow looked older and more energetic at once.

"Uncle," he said.

The auric king's eyes flicked from his screen to the road ahead of him, and back again. I noticed my mouth hanging open and shut it.

"You have spurned your right to call me by that name," the king said at length, then turned his black eyes on me. "If this is a ransom attempt, you will find no acquiescence here."

"No, uncle," Tribe cut off any response I might have had, which was just as well, as I was speechless. "He's right. Karthax is going to poison the water supply as soon as you take the city. He's had me in the VPen trying to get information out of me, until the Nightpath came."

The auric king's scowl softened for a moment, and his screen froze as he presumably checked our information. I looked up at Alina, whose eyes were as big as saucers.

Double-U Tee Eff, she mouthed at me.

I raised my hands, shrugging incredulously.

Thog'run's screen unfroze after a moment, and he looked even more dour, if it were possible.

"Your information is correct, Nightpath Aradowsi. We will have the traitors neutralized momentarily. And you, disobedient one," his eyes flicked to the part of his screen displaying my vision. I looked at Tribe, who met my gaze steadily.

"Return to Aurichome when this is over. I would have a word with you."

The digitab clicked as the king disconnected the call. The room collectively exhaled, most of us having forgotten to breathe. I eyed Tribe suspiciously, voicing the question on everyone's minds.

"Uncle?"

He wriggled nervously under my gaze. "He took me and my brother in when we first joined the revs. We were kids, and Aurichome was still a warzone. I got mixed up with the wrong crowd, started selling Oxidium, then doing it. He kicked me out. That was fifteen years ago."

"Wow. Didn't see that one coming," Vasshka's voice came through the digitab.

I vacillated, knowing that we needed to get moving but intrigued by the turn of events. None of my records had given any indication of Tribe's familial connection to the auric king, but I wasn't Karthax or the Sigil.

Madge, who had impassively watched the exchange, caught my eye. "Interesting friends you've made this week," she said, raising an eyebrow.

"You're telling me."

I brought the image of the VPen back up on my digitab, displaying it to the others. "We need to get out of here," I said, changing the subject. "If Thog'run's taking care of the utilities core, we can focus on intercepting Karthax and the Destroyer before they escape, and getting Striker to medical."

"We'll focus on not dying," Gloric said.

"Great."

"What about the ragers?" Alina asked.

I pursed my lips, thinking. "We could fight our way through, but we don't have the time." I turned to Madge. "Where would Karthax go?"

The Daypath responded without hesitation. "If he's hurt, they will have teleported to his sanctum to patch themselves up. If they know that Thog'run is in on their betrayal, they'll be getting to his airpad a-sap."

I nodded, bringing up the layout of the NIGHT facility to show it to the group. Karthax's sanctum and airpad were in the northern spire, requiring us to retrace our steps to the atrium and across to a separate set of elevators. Medical was south, also requiring entry into the central foyer. Alina, Madge and I might have been able to make it without arousing suspicion, but not in our bloodied state. Having Tribe and a sparkle-encrusted, comatose Striker wouldn't help.

Inspiration struck as I looked at the facility layout. "We can use the ragers as a distraction," I said.

"How so?" Tribe asked, still sitting in his chair.

"We can draw as many of them as we can into the maintenance stairwell and set them loose in the atrium," I explained, tracing my finger on the map. "Whatever agents are left will have their hands full. The rest of you can use the elevator to get up to medical."

"Rest of you? Where are you going?" Alina said.

I made an appealing gesture with my hands. "Someone has to persuade the ragers."

The Pitcher looked at me incredulously, clearly thinking me insane. Even Tribe gave me an appraising look, letting out a low whistle. He seemed to slowly be getting back to his normal self.

"I'm the only shadowmancer here," I put forward. "Tribe is in no condition to fight, and

Madge will need to be present to transport Striker with the stasis field."

"I could come with you," Alina offered.

I shook my head. "I can't hide you."

She nodded, understanding, but not liking it.

Madge put her hand on my shoulder, her grip firm. "Let us know when."

We prepared ourselves for battle, and I gave Alina directions on how to use her digitab's stolen profile to work the elevator's security system. I crushed a ceridium capsule and enveloped myself in a shadow shroud, standing by the door.

I looked back at the little party, who gazed vaguely in my direction. Tribe was busy flushing his Oxidium down the toilet, and Madge was using her stasis spell to lift Striker off of the floor. Alina stood quietly, fidgeting with her ceridium sphere and looking small.

"Buy you a beer when this is all over," I said to her, my heart in my throat.

She smiled, and it was the most brilliant thing I had ever seen, eclipsing the light coming off of Madge's spell. The expression reminded me of how fragile they were, and what easy targets they would make. I would have to draw as many ragers away from them as I could.

I clicked a button on my digitab, and disappeared through the doorway, shutting it again behind me.

The VPen was cold and oppressive as before, but wild noises punctured the air, echoing across the cavern's walls. The ragers were conscious and looking for a way out, howling, snarling, tearing at the stone and concrete. I shuddered, thinking about what they might have done to the VPen inhabitants they had already found.

"You're crazy, Nightpath," Gloric said into my ear, reading my mind. The gnome had found a dark place and was hiding with Vasshka, Buster, and a number of revolutionaries.

"Takes one to know one," I whispered. I crept around the bunker, keeping close to the wall, a wraith among shadows. Following the sounds of the closest screeches, I found the first group of ragers not far away, crouched like animals and arguing unintelligibly with one another.

The sight of them turned my stomach. Fear, revulsion, and pity vied for supremacy in my aching body, and I felt my injuries momentarily through the Oxadrenalthaline. I pushed the emotions away and drew my pistol and nightblade.

Five ragers squatted weirdly, fighting amongst themselves over some perceived or real threat. They yipped and snarled inhumanely, their hair knotted messes and what remained of their clothes in tatters.

I took a deep breath and leveled my pistol at one of the closest monsters, a lanky auric with broken tusks jutting from his mouth. I fired one shot, grazing his upper arm and sending him sprawling into the crowd. They fought over him for a minute and then turned slowly in my direction, searching for the intruder.

The looks on their faces will haunt me to the end of my days. Cold, lifeless eyes scoured the air around me, their sweaty visages twisted in unrelenting anger. Their heightened vision would ordinarily be able to pick me out in the dim light, but because of my shadow shroud, all they would have seen was two floating, cobalt-laced weapons.

One of them, a tiny female, snarled, and the group leapt to their feet, their superhuman strength making them move unreasonably quickly. The sight of my weapons sent them into a frenzy, exacerbating their already antagonized state. Even the auric I had shot stumbled towards me, oblivious to the wound on his arm.

I ran, trailing the sword behind me as a goad for the ragers. They hooted and hollered, bounding after me, and I raced behind another bunker, retracting my nightblade and stuffing my pistol back in my coat. I kept running, hearing the monsters grunt confusedly as they turned around the corner. I gave myself several paces of a head start, then drew my glowing sword again, hearing the ragers scream in protest in response and give chase.

I continued to weave in between cells, drawing and sheathing my sword, guiding the ragers through the VPen like a minotaur in a labyrinth. Here and there, I encountered other little groups, who joined the chase, building a motley crew of pursuers in my wake.

I worked my way towards the rear of the VPen, hiding my nightblade and fumbling with my digitab. Spotting the maintenance shaft ahead, I activated the stairwell's digital locking mechanism from afar, seeing the reinforced metal door open in front of me no more than twenty yards away.

I accelerated into a sprint, turning for a second to ensure the ragers were still on my trail. They were. Over thirty of them were caterwauling down the hallway, running, leaping, or galloping on four limbs. I didn't know whether to be excited or terrified.

As I reoriented myself towards the stairwell, a rager stepped out from a nearby cell, drawn by the noise. I bumbled into him, tumbling to the floor and nearly dropping my digitab. He took the blow with a confused grunt and fell on his back, clawing at the air around me. I turned the fall into a roll and kept running, redrawing my sword to guide the monsters into the maintenance shaft.

I bolted through the doorway, hastily stashing my nightblade and pulling out my pistol. With two well-placed shots, I took out the shaft's overhead lights, casting the current floor in darkness, broken only by the glow of my gun and digitab. Knowing the ragers were right on my tail, I sprinted up the stairs, trusting my shadow shroud to keep me invisible save for my weapons.

The monsters barreled into the stairwell a moment later, filling the space with their battered, foul-smelling bodies, ripping at one another, searching for the source of their pursuit. It took a few seconds for them to spot my pistol, disappearing up the steps. One of them howled, and I jumped despite myself, the sound reverberating deafeningly upon the concrete walls.

I turned the corner on a switchback in the shaft, almost at the second underground level of the facility. A landing loomed ahead, lit by two well-placed lights in the stairwell. I fired at them with my pistol, taking the steps two at a time and racing around another corner towards the upper levels.

As I puffed up the stairs, I could feel the ragers coming dangerously close behind me, and knew that I had miscalculated either their speed or my energy levels. I frantically tapped at the digitab, opening the portal up the next flight of stairs that would lead into a corridor adjacent to the Gressler Atrium. Drawing upon my body's exhausted reserves, I dashed to the next landing, firing at another set of lights and pocketing my pistol and digitab.

I'm not proud of what I did next. I pressed myself up against the first underground floor landing's metal door, seeing the ragers advance up the shaft towards me. Their angry momentum would carry them upstairs towards the next lighted platform and into the atrium, but there was no telling if one or more of them would notice me as they passed my hiding place.

The ragers came up the stairwell like a wave of fire ants, yelling unintelligibly at one another and tearing at the steps and walls around them. They came onto the little landing, bumping into me and continuing on to the next set of stairs. I knew their augmented senses would allow them to smell me in the confined area, so I made myself very small, crouching under my shadow shroud with my hands over my head and thinking angry thoughts. I willed myself to be one of them for as long as they were in the maintenance shaft, hiding in the darkness and allowing their grubby limbs to brush against me, their stench my best disguise.

It was the longest thirty seconds I had experienced. The ragers poured ever upwards, spitting, scratching, and salivating around me. They bumped into me with their filthy legs, their long, dirt-encrusted fingernails scratching my clothes and arms. I gagged at the smell, a mixture of sweat, blood, excrement, and other foul things.

After what seemed like an eternity, they were gone, their voices echoing across the walls as they left the stairwell and entered the corridor and atrium beyond. I followed them, running up the flight of stairs to see the last of them spill through the open door like fetid air through a pressure valve. The sweet smell of marble and air conditioning wafted in towards me as the ragers scampered into the atrium, running in every direction and yapping like hyenas. The few agents present desperately reached for their weapons or took off, yelling into their digitabs.

It didn't take long for the alarm to sound, and voices started blaring instructions over the PA system. I used the distraction to dart out of the shaft and around a corner into the atrium, soaking in the relatively fresh air and tracing the rounded wall to the north corridor.

"Coast is clear," I spoke into my microphone. "There might be a few more down there, so be careful."

"Gotcha," Alina spoke into my ear. "We're heading out. Good luck, Nightpath."

"You too."

I glided around the room, unconcerned about being spotted amidst the mayhem. The ragers were throwing themselves after a handful of retreating agents and scurrying down the hallways leading off of the atrium. The facility was a cacophony of monster screams, human yells, and ceridium weaponry against a constant backdrop of blaring alarms and droning speakerphones. The normally well-lit area was bathed in circulating red lamps, alerting anyone present that the facility was under attack.

I followed a pair of ragers, a dwarf and a gnome, down the north hall to a set of three freestanding elevators, watching the monsters separate around the structures and continue deeper into the facility. Using my digitab and Gloric's enabled access codes, I hailed the central elevator and took it to its penultimate level, brushing my clothes with my hands in a feeble attempt to rid myself of the rager smell.

The elevator pulled into the upper reaches of the tower, and as the doors opened I stuck to its side panel, out of sight of the room beyond. The antechamber to Karthax's sanctum and airpad would be guarded, even with the battle broiling across the Bay and ragers penetrating throughout the facility below. I held a button on my digitab to keep the doors ajar, listening.

A distant voice reverberated from the room. "Sir, the elevator opened behind you. It appears empty. Are you expecting others?"

There was a pause as the man listened to a response within his earpiece. I recognized the voice - Beren Furghast, Lieutenant Inquisitor and one-time friend. I had no way of knowing if he was loyal to Karthax or if I could sway him to come to my side. I wouldn't have time for an extended conversation, and was unsure of my ability to sneak my way past him.

"Understood," his voice carried into the elevator. "I'll lock it down."

There was a shuffling as Furghast armed himself. "Wait here," he said to someone.

I released the button on the digitab and stashed the device in my coat, allowing the elevator to begin to close. I could hear the Inquisitor's footfalls grow louder and quicker as he raced towards the vault, sticking his pistol arm in between the doors to keep them from shutting. Seeing my opportunity, I grabbed his wrist, pulling him into the doors before they slid apart and knocking the gun out of his hand. He sank, unconscious, to the floor as the elevator reopened, and I ducked back out of view.

"The hell?" a woman's voice called. I didn't recognize her. "Beren!"

I heard her start chanting a spell, and spun out of the elevator into the room, drawing and aiming my stunner. The woman, a young Daypath, was moving her arms in opposing circles, delaying her spell until the attacker appeared. I had the benefit of the shroud that would obscure her vision, but she would be ready to fire at any movement.

She was fast, but I was faster. She let loose her spell, flinging a bolt of pure radiance at my shadowy form. The arrow crackled with energy as it tore through the air, and I had just enough time to twist out of the way and fire my stunner. The woman grabbed at her face as she fell backwards, jerking with electricity.

I holstered my weapon and hurried into the room, a corporate-looking entrance hall with lush seats and several doorways leading off into the tower's surrounding chambers. A glass wall stood directly ahead, watermarked fashionably with the insignia of the NIGHT organization and the Great Seal of the United States. I ran over to the open door inset into the wall, stepping carefully over the unconscious Daypath and into Karthax's sanctum.

For the office of one of the most powerful military leaders in the world, it wasn't much to look at. Like the man, the room was stark, with very few pictures adorning the concrete walls and a simple wooden desk with the Inquisitor General's monitor setup. Several chairs were placed neatly about the room, and a long bearskin rug was the office's only ornamentation.

If I had stopped to think about it, I would have found the irony of Karthax's sanctum amusing. It was austere, and visible to anyone from the antechamber. An architectural statement that the Inquisitor General had nothing to hide, which was wholly at odds with the truth.

I rushed through the room to a short flight of steps leading to another glass wall that enclosed the northernmost side of the tower from the outside world. A large landing jutted out over the island below, brightly lit against the night sky, with a ceridium-powered copter sitting in the center of it. Karthax, bandaged from the waist up, was being helped into the vehicle by Agrid the Destroyer, who himself had his injured arm wrapped. The Inquisitor General moved slowly but was very much mobile.

I pulled out my digitab and unlocked the door set in the wall, ripping it open and immediately being assaulted by the wind and the noise of the copter's blades. Having helped Karthax into the pilot's seat, the Destroyer turned towards me, his maroon coat flapping crazily behind him. I stashed my digitab and drew my pistol and nightblade, firing first at the assassin and then at Karthax. The entromancer deflected my shot with a wave of his hand, and my ceridium bullets ricocheted harmlessly off of the copter's reinforced armor.

Desperate, I dropped my shadow shroud and any pretense of stealth with it, and ran headlong towards the Destroyer, firing shot after shot towards him and the copter. The aggressiveness took the assassin by surprise, and he frantically deflected and dodged my attacks, drawing his spear in between movements. I closed the distance between us and thrust at him with my sword, tearing a hole in his overcoat.

He backed away from me, dangerously close to the platform's unprotected perimeter. I used the movement to level my pistol at Karthax, who was exposed through the copter's open door. The Inquisitor General was ready for it, his hands and eyes burning with silver fire. I shot at him, but the fire ate the bullet and snaked towards me, wrapping around my pistol. I dropped it hastily and twisted out of the way.

The timing was perfect, as the Destroyer's spear bit the air where I had just been standing. Karthax jerked the door of the copter closed as I pivoted in place, slashing towards the assassin horizontally. He parried it with the butt of the spear and thrust towards me. I didn't have time to dodge the attack and took it in the solar plexus, pain bursting through my body and the wind escaping from my lungs. I managed to move out of the way as the entromancer continued the riposte, slashing down with the blade of the spear, but he still nicked my jaw, drawing blood.

The copter teetered, beginning to leave the platform. I wavered on my feet, grabbing at my chest and feigning as though I was going to double over. The auric took the bait, striking at me with his glowing spear in what would have been a killing blow. I dodged out of the way, slithering past his guard and smashing a ceridium capsule I had snatched from my coat into his face. I spat a word, and the sleep spell escaped my fingers and into his mind. His eyes rolled back in his head and his knees sagged, but he fought against the magic, shaking himself awake.

The distraction was all that I needed. I continued moving past him and kicked the back of his knee, dropping him to the floor. I followed his motion with my sword, letting the tip of it rest against his neck.

I booted the spear from his hand over the platform, letting it fall to the island far below. The copter whipped my hair and coat as it rose, and I stared daggers at Karthax through the machine's windows. He met my gaze, expressionless, knowing that the Destroyer's life was in my hands. Then he lifted the copter away from the tower and east over the Bay.

The platform was eerily silent in the vacuum left by the whirring copter. The wind continued to gust at us, but I could hear the Destroyer's heavy breath over the sound.

"So that's how it is, is it?" I looked down at him, tipping my head at the receding copter.

The auric shrugged under my sword, unflinching. "I would do the same."

"I guess you would," I said. "Gloric?" The gnome's vision on my display was dark.

"Waiting for you to be done so we can get out of here," he said into my ear.

"Great," I replied. "Get the revs to send a copter up to Karthax's airpad, and a security transporter. We'll have a guest."

"Got it," he said.

"Alina?" I asked.

"In the elevator," the Pitcher said. I was relieved to hear her voice. "Be up in medical in no time."

"Avoid the atrium if you can," I instructed. "It's kind of a mess."

I stared down at the Destroyer, who was looking at me curiously.

"What is it?" I asked him, keeping my nightblade against his neck.

"You're weak," he said.

"Says the guy on the floor?"

He smirked, white tusks gleaming against his pale face. Then he grabbed my sword by the blade, cutting into his hand but wrenching the weapon out of the way as he rolled to his feet. The sudden movement knocked me off balance, and I stumbled forward as the entromancer cast out his hand, spraying blood towards me and stamping his foot, grinding his teeth together with a growl. The droplets elongated into crimson arrows, hurtling towards me from point blank range.

I had nowhere to go but forward, feeling the agony of arrows tearing through my left shoulder and leg but crashing into him, driving my nightblade through his torso and sending us both sprawling towards the edge of the platform. He rolled backwards, putting his foot in my abdomen and sending me flying. I managed to catch him with my knee in the jaw before I flew over him, skittering along the concrete. I banged painfully off of a metal light bolted to the floor and slid over the platform.

I grabbed the floor lamp with my good hand, struggling to slow my momentum. My left arm wouldn't respond, and I could feel my right arm threatening to pull out of its socket under the pressure. The lamp creaked but held, and I found myself dangling off of the platform, a hundred feet from the ground.

The wind buffeted me against the concrete, cold and merciless. My left arm and leg were numb, and the rest of me was on fire, the Oxadrenalthaline unable to keep up with all of the injuries. Spikes of agony shuddered down my right arm, which held precariously onto the lamp.

There is a frame of mind that few humans or aurics reach without the use of Oxidium or other stimulants. It is fueled by the will to survive when there is no other recourse, when one's back is against the wall and there is nothing left to lose. It is a feeling forged in the fires of anger, hammered at the anvil of determination, and wielded by a consciousness that doesn't know the meaning of failure.

It's also known as adrenaline.

I flexed my right arm, dragging myself up the side of the platform, feeling blood soil my clothing. With a sheer force of will, I swung my left arm over the concrete, screaming in pain as I shuffled unceremoniously over the lip and onto the relative safety of the airpad.

I crawled at first, pushing myself to my knees and stumbling to my feet, holding my left arm against my body. I limped over to the Destroyer, who was lying on his side, my sword sticking out weirdly from his body. My leg pulsed in pain as I bent over, examining him.

His eyes fluttered open, and they were raw with pain. He lifted a hand weakly, and I kicked it away, almost falling over myself. I grabbed the sword and pulled it out of him, eliciting a grunt.

"You should have killed me," he wheezed.

"I still might," I said, bashing the hilt of the blade into his temple. He rolled over onto his back, unconscious.

I stood there, bleeding, catching my breath. The sky was still dark, but I noticed for the first time since entering the airpad the brilliance of the city to the west. It was bright with building lights, neon signs, and a few burning explosions here and there. By dawn, it would belong to Thog'run.

I sheathed my sword, clearing my throat. "Gloric," I said into the night, "be sure to send a healer."

TWELVE

We have neither the military might nor the political acumen to challenge the NIGHTs on their doorstep, yet we need neither. We need only look to the truth in our minds and the certainty of our hearts to know that one day, they will answer for their crimes against the aurics of our great country. And that answer shall be heard across the planet, so that one name will be pronounced among all of the realms that have sought to oppress our fathers, our mothers, our brothers, our sisters, our children. And that name will be Aurichome.

-Thog'run II, King of Aurichome

Thog'run's summons took about a week to reach me. I had done something unorthodox and gone completely off of the grid, hiding in my apartment and watching reruns of forties' holovids while my wounds healed. Reheated flash-frozen meals had never tasted so good.

The city, now under auric control, had changed immeasurably and not at all. The blue and white colors of Aurichome now decorated City Hall, the bridges, and most of the other recognizable monuments. Over a hundred underrace communities in the United States and several small nations formally swore fealty to Thog'run, forcing the American government to reconsider its stance towards Aurichome, tentatively opening the channels for a parley. A celebration was scheduled for the following week to inaugurate the reopening of the Golden Gate, and Thog'run's conquest of the West Bay, from Skaggs Island to Pacifica, was now complete.

Regimes may change, but people don't. After Karthax fled San Francisco, the Pacific South NIGHTs were without a leader, and either retreated to Alcatraz, were captured, or blew town to seek refuge at Pacific North in Seattle. The mayor, knowing without question which way the wind was blowing, obsequiously and publicly gave Thog'run the key to the city, a ludicrous gesture given that the auric king had already assumed power through force. Yet, for all the media vamping and political commentary that ensued, the city was still standing, the trains continued to not run on time, and people returned to their daily lives.

When I finally re-enabled the network on my digitab, I had over a hundred messages waiting for me, mostly from independent media agencies wanting the full story of my attempted assassinations, the Inquisitor General's multiple betrayals, and what was colloquially being called "Ragegate 2076." Gloric had uploaded the video and audio from my lens recordings onto the network, and they had gone viral. We were all of us celebrities overnight, though none of us embraced it as fully as the gnome, who had private corporations approaching him left and right to volley for his technomancy against their competitors. Even Alina's name was cleared somewhat, demonstrating that while she wasn't on the all-American side of the fence that was expected of her, she was still on the ethical one.

Only a handful of the messages were from people I knew, with several from Madge and Gloric, and one from Alina. The Daypath had been hastily elected as the interim Inquisitor General by the NIGHT council at large, which was more of an attempt at saving face than anything truly repentant. Karthax's collusion with the auric king, coercion and torture of NIGHT and revolutionary forces, and near-assassination of multiple agents looked really bad, and the NIGHT leadership was quick to pillory the former Inquisitor General as an independent actor. They stripped him of his rank *in absentia,* promoted Madge without her having any Inquisitor experience, and opened up official lines of communication with

Aurichome so that the Alcatraz facility could remain in operation.

I opened the message from Alina, which had a simple note: *Thog'run wants to see us. Tomorrow, 11PM, Aurichome. Pick you up at 9.*

It had been sent yesterday, giving me less than an hour to get ready for an official audience with the king.

I quickly showered, shaved, and changed into a clean set of clothes, three things I hadn't done in a week and hadn't realized I had been missing. I holstered my weapons and a good amount of ceridium capsules, tugging on my coat as I hurried down the twelve flights to street level.

Alina was already waiting for me, her black SUV double-parked in the alley behind my apartment building in Silver Terrace. Gloric sat chatting with her in the front seat, so I pulled open the rear door and jumped in, being greeted laconically by Vasshka and more warmly by a freshly-brushed Buster.

"Where's Tribe?" I asked after we exchanged pleasantries and were on our way.

"He's already there," Alina explained, taking us onto the freeway and the Bay Bridge beyond.

The evening traffic was a nightmare, and we were grateful for the SUV's antigravity boosters, which allowed us to keep moving, albeit slowly, over the bridge and north through the East Bay. I wondered irritably why Thog'run had chosen to delay the long-anticipated re-opening of the Golden Gate, but supposed he had his own priorities.

As we drove, my friends caught me up on their activities and that of the outside world over the past week. Alina had initiated the long, grueling process of rebuilding *They Might Be Giant*, and had received the open support of the underrace community for what was to be their official taproom in San Francisco. Gloric was up to his considerably large ears in media and business requests, being not only one of the heroes of Ragegate but also the Captain of the Sigil. Vasshka had taken a trip to Mystic to pay her respects to her brother, and returned with renewed vigor for what had once been the revolutionary cause. She remained a gun for hire, but her allegiance was exclusively to Aurichome.

I was delighted to hear that Striker had made a full recovery, Alina's terramancy and Madge's stasis spell keeping him alive until he was able to get proper medical attention. The human would wear a metal breastplate and use a mechanical arm for the rest of his days, but he would live to irritate other NIGHTs until he pissed off someone else. The thought made me smirk.

As for Tribe, my companions informed me that he had indeed returned to Thog'run, patching things up with his surrogate uncle and taking a seat at his side as a prince of Aurichome. The king had several biological children and relatives of his own, so there was no danger of the frivolous auric becoming sovereign someday, but it was still a step up in the world.

Reluctantly, I asked about Agrid the Destroyer, feeling guilty in my hopeful speculation that he may have succumbed to his wounds after the copter took us away from Alcatraz. Vasshka explained that he was in the king's custody, which, if the stories of Thog'run's behavior towards his enemies were to be believed, would not prove to be restorative to the entromancer's well being.

The assassin may have been right after all. I should have killed him.

We took the 580 west through Richmond and over the newly named Aurichome - Richmond Bridge into the North Bay, stopping briefly at an auric checkpoint to verify our identification. Alina took us off the freeway and followed several local roads into the forest, the neighborhoods around us slowly changing from coastal suburbs to rural encampments. Our route led us into the woods and eventually underground, into the warrens underneath Aurichome.

It was my first time in the underrace nation, and although I had seen pictures of the country, no images or holovids could do justice to the real experience. Compared to the incessant bustle of the city, the forest and underground were positively tranquil, rugged landscapes that blended country living with bleeding edge technology. Elegantly carved stone walls surrounded the road we traversed, and shops cunningly built into the sides of the tunnel stood closed but bright with neon AR advertisements. The structures were still new but boasted the best of auric stonework, and I wondered what the aboveground forest cities looked like during the daytime.

We made our way through several subterranean neighborhoods, my companions making small talk while I gawked like a tourist. There were quite a few cars and pedestrians at this time of night, aurics returning to their homes and carousers making their rounds at various pubs and nightclubs. It wasn't the buzz of New Castro or downtown, but it had the feel of a living, breathing city nonetheless.

Alina drove us through a gigantic rotary with a huge stone statue at its heart and several spokes leading off into different directions. The sculpture, a twenty foot monstrosity carved from limestone, sandstone, and granite, depicted Thog'run in all of his glory, his foot placed triumphantly on the throat of a coiled dragon and his axe lifted for the killing blow. Yellow and white lights ensured that the statue was the focal point of anyone entering the roundabout, and small fountains sprayed at intervals opposite the roads.

We took a northerly passage, driving deeper into Aurichome and coming to another checkpoint. The troll at the guardpost took one look at our credentials and waved us through, into another cavern that dwarfed that of the rotary. Four roads led into the cavern from opposite directions, diverting around a central square. The cave's single establishment was a squat, severe-looking building that was imposing in its austerity, situated at the center of the square. It was evidently still in construction, as scaffolding encircled the entire western wing of the structure, but long blue and white pennants sprouted proudly from the marble walls.

We parked at a small lot near the south side of the cavern, leaving the paved street for a marble walkway that led into the king's palace. Auric guards were stationed at intervals, looking all the more dangerous in the half-light of the cavern's street lamps. Very few people populated the area at this time, but there were still a number of officials bustling about the square, and a handful of tourists attempting to capture holovids of the structure.

Wide stone stairs rose up to the palace, leading us to a third checkpoint in front of the building's troll-sized wooden doors, which stood open. Four auric guards stood in the livery of the king, flanking the portal. A fifth guard, a gnome, examined our IDs carefully before allowing us to proceed.

Two of the king's guard detached themselves from the entryway and followed us into the palace, silent sentries who matched our pace. We entered a large, unadorned vestibule whose only decoration was a simple Aurichome flag stuck in the middle of the marble floor. Ceridium-powered construction lamps stood at intervals, bathing the vestibule in soft cold light, and passageways led to the north and east wings. The west passage was blocked with yellow construction tape.

We followed the north entrance into a cavernous auditorium, a thick blue and white carpet softening our footfalls. The room was considerably more furnished than its antechamber, with augmented reality paintings projecting images of Thog'run I and II and their families, historic underrace battle scenes, and Aurichome in various states of construction. A dozen chandeliers hung from the vaulted ceiling, creating an equal amount of light and shadows, and rows of stone pews lined both sides of the carpeted walkway.

I exchanged a look with Alina, who lifted an eyebrow playfully in response. Buster led our little party proudly forward, and Gloric and Vasshka sauntered comfortably behind. I seemed to be the only one who was nervous.

A small, oval dais was built into the northernmost wall of the room, with two curving staircases hugging it on either side. The front of the platform stuck out like a prow into the auditorium, no more than six feet tall, but requiring anyone approaching the back of the room to split off onto one of the staircases. A podium stood at the fore of the dais, allowing a speaker to address the room and be easily seen by all.

One of the king's guard moved in front of Buster and guided us up the leftmost stairs while the other auric brought up the rear. We walked up onto the dais, which extended back forty feet to a little reception area decorated in blue and white. Sapphire and cream curtains were roped to the walls, providing a little color in the ascetic room, and the dim ceiling lights turned the blue carpet underneath a deep azure. The sharp smell of stone was offset by a small metal brazier that held burning incense.

A small party awaited us at the end of the dais, chatting quietly among themselves. Thog'run II sat patiently atop a raised marble and sandstone throne, his giant hand resting on the head of a battleaxe. To either side of him stood several family members and functionaries, all eyeing us cautiously. I recognized his wife, Fazgha Hezdottr, and their firstborn, Thog'run III, hovering protectively next to the throne, and one or two dignitaries.

Tribe was one of many aurics, standing the furthest away from the king, but dressed in fine clothing of royal colors. A half-ring of guards stood around them all.

The king's guard walked to within ten feet of the royal party and stopped, saluting Thog'run with a fist in the air. The king returned the gesture, and the guard moved to the side, mirrored by his compatriot behind us. We spread out in a line in front of the party, who had stopped talking at our approach.

Gloric and Vasshka dropped to a knee, followed by Alina. I caught Tribe's eye with mine, and the thief smiled slightly, inclining his head towards the king. I glanced back at Thog'run, who looked on amusedly, wondering what I would do. Never one to be outdone by my companions, I took a knee, sweeping my coat out behind me.

"Rise, guests of Aurichome," the king said with a chuckle. "And be welcome."

We stood, except for Buster, who fell asleep at Alina's feet. I shuffled from one foot to the other, self-conscious under the gaze of the royal party. My friends didn't seem to mind the attention.

"So," Thog'run continued, "this is the Nightpath who has caused me so much trouble, only to deliver the city to me in the swiftest victory I have yet won."

The king's voice boomed from the throne, but he sat stock still, a giant upon the massive stone chair. His jaw moved, but his body didn't, and his hand never left the battleaxe propped on the floor. He might as well have been carved from the same marble as the throne.

I am not often intimidated by people, aurics or otherwise. I have wrestled trolls, fought off assassins, and been hunted by all manner of humans and beasts. Yet, in the presence of the auric king, I felt a strong urge to bow, flee, or a combination of the two, simply by virtue of his bearing and implicit command. He was huge, the grey muscles of his powerful arms naked from the shoulder down. His blue and white tabard and brown pants were tight on his stocky body, and a simple gold circlet sat atop his massive head, placed neatly around his long topknot.

It wasn't his size, posture, or even the enormous battleaxe that impressed me. Nor did his distinctive face, with its protruding brow, menacing tusks, and strangely humanoid snout frighten me. What pierced me to my core, exhorting me to kneel or flee, were his eyes.

They were black, but not the flat emptiness found in a shark's lifeless orbs. The king's eyes were obsidian pools that were hard and calculating while still emanating pride and command. As I met his gaze, I felt that I was being laid bare in front of him, each part of my physical and mental form appraised and catalogued for another time. Not many could hold his scrutiny, and I nearly faltered, recognizing why so many humans and aurics alike continued to swear fealty in his presence. I had thought him imposing in our video call, but meeting him in person was a different thing entirely.

I managed to hold his stare, and realized awkwardly that he was waiting for me to respond. Not knowing what to say, I stupidly raised my fist in the Aurichome salute.

I could see Vasshka glare at me from the corner of my eye, but the king returned the gesture. "Tell me, Nightpath Eskander Aradowsi," he said, "how you managed to defeat the Inquisitor General and his lackey, Agrid the Betrayer."

A dozen platitudes came to mind, unquestionably dug up from the tripe that one hears passively from commentators during televised sports games. I tried to keep it simple. "They underestimated us," I said, opening my hands to include the group.

"They were not alone in that," Thog'run rumbled, shifting his grip on the battleaxe. Slowly, the king rose from the throne, the light glinting from his eyes and tusks as he moved. Ponderously, he stepped down from the little platform upon which the throne sat, his heavy footfalls audible even on the thick carpet. His movements were slow but smooth, as though each step were precisely calculated. He reminded me vaguely of the Destroyer, but far more powerful.

The ring of guards parted as he advanced towards us, and Thog'run nonchalantly handed the battleaxe to an auric on his right as he approached. The king's wife and firstborn peeled away from the royal party to follow him, standing slightly behind.

The king of Aurichome stopped in front of me, towering over me by a head and a half. He was well over six feet tall and as thick as a NIGHT double-cruiser, eclipsing the throne and people behind him. It took every ounce of will that I had to not take a step backwards.

"It seems that I owe you an apology, Nightpath Aradowsi," he rumbled, "for thinking of you as collateral damage in my collusion with the Inquisitor General, rather than the savior of our people."

I licked my lips nervously. "It was nothing," I said modestly.

"On the contrary!" the king boomed, smiling a little. His breath smelled like cardamom. "Were it not for your efforts, and those of your companions," he swept a hand to include the group, "we most of us would have perished in the worst way possible, according to the Inquisitor General's machinations."

I bowed slightly, not knowing what to say.

"You have delivered the city into my hands, and my nephew-" the king inclined his head in Tribe's direction, "-home. For these deeds, I am in your debt."

I shuffled in place, feeling the weight of my friends' eyes on me.

Then Thog'run did something unanticipated. More swiftly than any motion he had made in our presence, he thrust out a hand expectantly in my direction.

I looked sideways at my friends frantically for support, being completely out of my depth. Finding no forthcoming suggestions, I offered my hand to the king.

Thog'run took it, still towering over me, his rough hand grasping my arm in a warrior's clasp. He leaned in towards me, smelling like herbs and sandalwood. "I am not used to misjudging people," he said dryly, and quietly, so only I could hear him. "Let's not make it a habit."

I nodded, understanding his statement. The king was not above apologizing for ordering my assassination, but would not hesitate to do it again if I proved untrustworthy.

He pulled away, releasing his grip on my arm and marched back up to the throne, collecting his battleaxe as he walked. Fazgha Hezdottr and Thog'run III followed in his wake after the king's firstborn gave me a long appraising glance. The guards and dignitaries stood patiently as the royal party passed them, murmuring in spite of themselves at our exchange.

Thog'run sat on his throne, resuming his statuesque position with his hand leaning on the battleaxe. He lifted his free arm, and Tribe soberly came forward from the shadows, sidling in between the ring of guards with a small pillow balanced on his palm. On it rested four small brooches, round platinum coins emblazoned with the seal of Aurichome atop tiny blue and white pennants.

The king spoke as Tribe began affixing the clasps to each of our jackets, starting with Gloric.

"The four of you shall now be known as friends to Aurichome. These clasps will identify you as such throughout the kingdom and the world beyond its doors. Their internal chips have been encrypted for authenticity."

Tribe stooped to offer a brooch to Vasshka, who gave him a companionable pat on his shoulder.

"Moreover," Thog'run continued, "my court has need for the likes of your skills, beginning with yours, Gloric Vunderfel."

For once, the gnome appeared surprised, looking up from fiddling with his new medallion. "Your Highness?" he said in a small voice.

The king graced him with a rare smile. "I would have you as my Chief of Technology, technomancer, if the Sigil would permit it."

"I...um," Gloric stammered, blushing uncharacteristically. "I...yes, Your Highness."

I shared a smirk with Tribe, who moved over to pin a pendant to my lapel. That would put bees in the bonnets of all of the corporations who were after Gloric for his technomancy. When the king asked, you didn't have much of a choice.

Thog'run nodded, turning his attention to Doubleshot. "Vasshka Lestrage," he grunted, "you have already sworn fealty to Aurichome, and I bid you continue in your service to the crown."

The dwarf bobbed her head solemnly, clenching her hand in salute. Belatedly, Gloric remembered the gesture, hastily copying Vasshka and putting his fist in the air.

The king skipped over me and spoke to Alina, who was receiving her pendant from Tribe. I was grateful for the reprieve from the court's attention.

"Alina Hadzic, Aurichome is in need of a liaison between its capital and the newly acquired territory. The Consulship is yours."

The Pitcher brightened, smoothing her new medallion against her chest. She saluted the auric king with the crispness of a soldier. "It would be my pleasure, Your Highness."

Tribe stood off to the side, holding the empty pillow, and I waited for the king to dismiss us.

He didn't. Thog'run turned towards me, a shrewd look in his hard eyes. "Nightpath Eskander Aradowsi," he rumbled, "I need a spymaster. One who knows the mind of humans but has the heart of an auric. And more importantly, one with the skills to uncover what other plots the Inquisitor General and Agrid the Betrayer may have put in motion, and quash them."

I hedged, feeling my palms wet and my mouth dry. Madge had made it clear to me that I still had a job at the NIGHT headquarters if I wanted it, but I had thought to give it more time before making a decision. My physical wounds were on the mend, but the psychological ones were a little too fresh.

"OK," I said dumbly, remembering to salute, and feeling instantly sorry for laughing at Gloric. When the king asked, you really didn't have a choice.

Thog'run saluted us all once again, and Tribe embraced us each in turn, returning to the shadows near his surrogate uncle. We knelt in appreciation, thanking the king for his audience.

"Go," he boomed, "and may Aurichome go with you."

My companions and I rose together, Alina nudging Buster with her foot to wake him. The wolf shook himself, panting happily.

We bid our goodbyes and walked down the curving steps and out of the audience chamber, the king's guards taking point and rear as before. They stayed at the entrance of the palace as we made our way back through the checkpoint and parking lot, chatting lightly about the night's turn of events.

"Drinks?" Alina asked as we got back in the car.

"I do owe you a beer," I said.

The others murmured their assent, and we took the long drive around the Bay and back into the city, each of us lost in thoughts of the past and future. Alina drove us to an underrace bar in SOMA, one of the few pubs still open after one in the morning.

Gloric and Vasshka walked up to the establishment, an edgy-looking place called *City Sparks*. I waited for Alina to lock the SUV, putting my hand on her arm as she began to follow the gnome and dwarf.

"Wait," I said hesitantly as she turned back towards me. Buster leaped ahead, knowing he wouldn't be allowed inside but excited by the din of the bar.

The Pitcher looked at me quizzically, a glint of mischief in her eyes. "What is it?"

"I just want," I coughed, embarrassed. "I haven't thanked you, for everything. For healing me, for coming with me, and for believing me."

She grinned impishly, the night wind blowing wisps of curly hair out from under her cap. "You still haven't."

I chuckled involuntarily, removing my hand from her wrist. "Thank you," I said simply.

"You're welcome, Nightpath," she replied, grabbing my hand in hers and pulling me towards the pub. Her grip was soft but strong.

I took a chance, and held onto her grasp, drawing her back towards me. She turned, surprised, but acquiesced into my grip.

I kissed her, putting my hand in the small of her back and holding her against my body. She melted just the tiniest bit in my arms, resting her palm on my chest. The sounds of the tavern wafted out into the wind around us, and traffic continued to move behind and above us.

I pulled away, opening my eyes and looking into hers, which were an incandescent shade of blue even at night. She bit her lip, smiling at my boldness.

"Call me Eskander," I said.

EPILOGUE

Agrid the Destroyer sat in his cell, staring at the stone wall in front of him. He shifted slightly on his wooden cot, ignoring the itching of his powerful hands trapped within the metal cylinder. The manacle restricted any fine motions of his fingers, and was latched to his ankles by a ceridium-laced cord. A reinforced kerchief of sorts, bound by steel and pocked with ceridium stones, was wrapped around his mouth and lower jaw, removed only when he was allowed to eat and surrounded by guards. Each of the bonds had been ensorcelled with anti-mancy spells, and any potential object that could be used for magical purposes had been removed from the otherwise stark chamber.

Though his hands and mouth were shackled, the entromancer yet worked. His eyes traced the subtle curvatures in the wall, memorizing the patterns and keeping his mind agile. He isolated each muscle in his body that was free from bondage, flexing and relaxing them to ensure they remained strong and flexible.

Above all, he *thought*, reviewing the countless number of spells in his repertoire, cataloging his memory of the past while calculating the possible outcomes of present and future. He sent his mind to the farthest reaches of the Earth, returning only to take care of his bodily needs at the prescribed times.

On a day that could have been any other, Agrid was wakened from his reverie at a non-appointed time, the reinforced metal door of his cell sliding into its stone casing with a whisper. As though pushing a button on a holovid, he paused the stream of his thoughts, turning his head slowly to see who had come to visit him. Despite his efforts, his neck muscles were stiff and sore from the lack of movement.

A solitary figure stood in the doorway, shadowed in the murky overhead light by an enormous hooded cloak that covered the person from head to thigh. The figure paused for a moment, then entered the room, allowing the door to close and lock them both in the chamber.

The entromancer smirked within his kerchief, turning his head back towards the wall and away from the newcomer. He waited for the person to walk over and touch a button on the side of the kerchief, which responded to a chip in the figure's hand, retracting the metal to rest on the side of Agrid's face. The entromancer flexed his jaw, grateful in spite of himself for the reprieve.

"Brother," he said wryly, his voice dry and scratchy from disuse. "I thought you'd never come."

The figure stood watching him, thinking within its hood. The entromancer waited patiently, staring at the stone.

After a long moment, the figure lifted huge hands up to the cloak's cowl, pulling it back in the privacy of the chamber. Yellow tusks gleamed in the meager light, a long topknot unfolding freely as the hood fell.

Agrid the Destroyer looked up at Thog'run expectantly, waiting for him to speak. The king continued to stare, his black eyes hard and unreadable.

"Indeed," Thog'run rumbled, his low voice booming in the small cell. Ponderously, the king pulled up a wooden chair, the room's only furniture save the cot and a small desk. He placed it in front of the Destroyer, close enough to be uncomfortable, and sat down heavily, his armor creaking quietly.

"We have much to discuss," the king said.

ABOUT THE AUTHOR

M. S. Farzan was born in London and grew up in the San Francisco Bay Area. He has written and worked for high-profile video game companies and editorial websites such as Electronic Arts, Perfect World Entertainment, Modus Games, and MMORPG.com, and has served as the Community Manager for games like *Dungeons & Dragons Neverwinter* and *Mass Effect: Andromeda*. He has trained in and taught Japanese martial arts for over fifteen years and has a Ph.D. in Cultural and Historical Studies of Religions.